A PLUME BOOK

THE EMPTY GLASS

J. I. BAKER is a contributing editor to *Condé Nast Traveler* and a former development editor at Time Inc. He has also worked at *Real Simple*, *Glamour*, and *Us Weekly*, and is a founding editor of *Time Out New York*. This is his first novel.

Praise for *The Empty Glass*

"J. I. Baker's . . . *The Empty Glass* reminds me of what [David] Lynch might have brought to the tale of the world's most tragic cracked actress: a sense of doom, of outside forces too strong and warped to defeat, and of the grotesqueries of Hollywood." —Christopher Schobert, *The Buffalo News*

"Haunting, harrowing Hollywood noir at its finest."
—Megan Abbott, author of *Dare Me*

"*The Empty Glass* comes rampaging out of the gate and keeps on roaring and roistering until the sad, salutary shock of its final pages. After I started, the vivid writing and the presence of the unhappy latter-day Marilyn Monroe kept me reading all the way to the end. I want to tell everyone within the sound of my voice to buy this splendid novel. It's really punchy and really good, and you really should read it." —Peter Straub, author of *In the Night Room*

"J. I. Baker takes a bold run into Cain and DeLillo territory and scores. *The Empty Glass* is chilled and redolent of a good gin martini, leaving you primed to order another." —Barry Gifford, author of *Wild at Heart*

"Stylishly written and perfectly paced, *The Empty Glass* is noir fiction reimagined for the modern era, a novel that is sharp, smart, and breathlessly fast-paced, yet somehow manages to convey the slow burn of an old regret. As such, it marks the auspicious debut of a new voice in American suspense."
—Thomas H. Cook, author of *Taken*

"[In *The Empty Glass*] Baker conjures a suitably paranoid atmosphere and crackling dialogue in this look at the seedy intersection of celebrity, politics, and power."
—*Booklist*

"*The Empty Glass* is riveting, brilliant, and endlessly fascinating. Writing from a wholly original perspective, J. I. Baker has combined the history and myth surrounding one of the most intriguing deaths of the last century and created a shocking, unputdownable thriller."

—Jason Starr, author of *The Craving*

"J. I. Baker has spun a gripping and pulse-pounding conspiracy. Smart, perfectly atmospheric, and ultimately heartbreaking, *The Empty Glass* is one not to miss. It will stay with you long after the final page."

—Andrew Gross, author of *15 Seconds* and coauthor of six #1 *New York Times* bestsellers with James Patterson

"[An] imaginative 1960s yarn." —*Us Weekly*

"Marilyn Monroe is dead . . . by suicide. So why does all the evidence suggest that she was murdered? Los Angeles County deputy coroner Ben Fitzgerald's relentless search for answers leads him down a dangerous path away from his sanity—and [he] takes readers along with him. . . . [A] totally credible imagining of [Monroe's] uncensored speech: breathy, sparingly punctuated, and a little bit lost . . . but Baker is totally in control, and watching him lead his hero along a precarious tightrope of reason is scary—and totally exhilarating."

—Nathalie Gorman, Oprah.com

"It's *L.A. Confidential* meets the Bio Channel with a little TMZ thrown in for fun." —*Elle*

"Baker imagines Marilyn Monroe's death through the eyes of the coroner. Mixing fact and theory, this taut thriller explores conspiracies around her as well as the official's own psychological turmoil." —*InStyle*

"James Ellroy fans will relish Baker's impressive first novel, a dark paranoid thriller . . . [Baker's] barbed prose makes a familiar story fresh."

—*Publishers Weekly* (starred review)

THE EMPTY GLASS

J. I. Baker

A PLUME BOOK

PLUME
Published by the Penguin Group
Penguin Group (USA) Inc., 375 Hudson Street,
New York, New York 10014, USA

USA / Canada / UK / Ireland / Australia / New Zealand / India / South Africa / China
Penguin Books Ltd, Registered Offices: 80 Strand, London WC2R 0RL, England
For more information about the Penguin Group visit penguin.com

First published in the United States of America by Blue Rider Press,
a member of Penguin Group (USA) Inc., 2012
First Plume Printing, 2013

The Library of Congress has catalogued the Blue Rider Press edition as follows:

Baker, J. I. (James Ireland).
The empty glass / J. I. Baker.
p. cm.
ISBN 978-0-399-15819-3 (hc.)
ISBN 978-0-14-219678-6 (pbk.)
1. Monroe, Marilyn, 1926–1962—Death and burial—Fiction.
2. Motion-picture actors and actresses—United States—Fiction. I. Title.
PS3602.A58645E47 2012 2012009187
813'.6—dc23

Printed in the United States of America
1 3 5 7 9 10 8 6 4 2

Original hardcover design by Amanda Dewey

PUBLISHER'S NOTE
This is a work of fiction. Names, characters, places, and incidents either are the product of the author's imagination or are used fictitiously, and any resemblance to actual persons, living or dead, businesses, companies, events, or locales is entirely coincidental.

For my parents

THE
EMPTY GLASS

The great enemy of the truth is very often not the lie—deliberate, contrived, and dishonest—but the myth—persistent, persuasive, and unrealistic.

—*John F. Kennedy*

Let's play murder—or divorce.

—*Marilyn Monroe*

1.

After a while, everything started to blur.

I felt that I'd spent hours, days, lying on the floor of this hotel room with my face against the wood and my eyes open wide as the air came through the vent near my head. The whoosh was all I heard—then the door closing, the keys in the lock, the footsteps on the floor stopping as I turned to see the patent leather shoes before my eyes, the stub of a cigarette dropped between them, burning.

And then there was the gun.

"Wake up." Captain Hamilton pushed the Smith & Wesson into my neck. "I want you to write me a letter."

I don't remember when or how I did it. The three (or was it four? Or five? Or ten? I don't remember) Nembutals had knocked me out. The captain was out of focus, going double.

He handed me the pen that she had used to write her own last words, and forced me to write mine. Reeling on the bed with his gun at my temple, I thought of the notes written on napkins and doors and windows and carpets that lined the shelves of Suicide Notes and Weapons. Now I was adding my own:

Take care of Max for me. Tell him that I loved him. Tell him that whatever else his father did, he loved his son.

"That's good, Delilah." He loomed over me. "Now you feel good?"

I nodded.

"Even better." He handed me the bottle.

I leaned forward, reached for the pills, and ended up with the gun. Ah, his shoulder had been injured, Doc. *You* know that.

I don't need to tell you that I shot him. I was on my back, elbows locked. He was bending down when the gun kicked, a black dime smoking on his chest. He reared, touched the hole, and stared at the fluid that glistened like oil on his finger. "Oh, I know what this is," he said as he fell.

I heard the sound his skull made.

I know what happens when you die.

You sigh and rub your forehead. "All right." You shake a Chesterfield from your pack and light it with a kitchen match. You drag and blow smoke to the ceiling fan with the bulb above the table, and I notice (not for the first time) how clammy and pitted your skin is. You're a big man, Doc, like an aging football player, with the face and waist of a small-town cop. "Let's go over this again," you say. You adjust your wire-rimmed glasses and check the notes that you are keeping in the book near the Sony reel-to-reel, lying on the desk like a suitcase, rolling at RECORD. "You shot him."

"In self-defense. You see the bandages. You gave me the Novril."

"Is it working?"

"For now."

You sit on one side of the table; I sit on the other. Between us, that reel-to-reel, a stack of used and unused seven-inch tapes, a glass ashtray, a vial of Novril, and your pack of Chesterfields. There is also a box with a label reading "Fitzgerald, Ben, Psych Eval." It contains what you call "the evidence":

1. The Smith & Wesson
2. A vial of Nembutal
3. A piece of notebook paper reading "Chalet 52" and "July 28"
4. A stained manila folder containing a number of 8 × 10 photographs
5. *Amahl and the Night Visitors*
6. A bag of ashes
7. A new red MEMORIES diary.

You pick up Item No. 1. "It had your fingerprints on it."

"Like I said, I shot him."

"Why?"

"Why did anyone do anything? Everything changed after she died."

"Who?"

"The actress. I've told you this already."

"Tell me again."

So I do:

"I woke to the sound of the knock on the door and sat up in the light from the neon sign that snaked along the wall outside the window," I say. "An empty carton of moo goo gai pan sat beside me; I hadn't thrown it out. I wasn't sure if I had dreamt the knock or actually heard it. I didn't have a phone—"

"Hang on." You are frowning. Something is wrong with the Sony. The wheels have stopped. You hit REWIND, then PLAY, and I hear my voice:

"—touched the hole, and stared at the fluid that glistened like oil on his finger—"

You hit STOP and look up at me. "Like oil?"

I nod.

"It glistened like *oil*, Ben?"

"It's a simile."

"Who do you think you are, Edna Ferber?"

But you can't hear my voice on the tape anymore. This is where the recording stopped. There is nothing but static. You make minor adjustments to the machine and try it again: REWIND, STOP, PLAY.

It doesn't work. You hit it with the heel of your hand.

REWIND, STOP, PLAY.

My voice: "Why did anyone do anything? Everything changed after she died."

You pause the tape and look at me. "Now pick up where you left off."

"Give me a cigarette first."

"I thought you quit."

"That was yesterday."

You give me a cigarette.

And a Novril, too: for the pain.

After a while, everything starts to blur.

"Tell the truth this time," you say.

"I already told you the truth."

"So tell it again."

SUNDAY, AUGUST 5, 1962

2.

I woke to the sound of the knock on the door and sat up in the light from the neon sign that snaked along the wall outside the window. An empty carton of moo goo gai pan sat beside me; I hadn't thrown it out. I wasn't sure if I had dreamt the knock or actually heard it. I didn't have a phone.

"Hello?"

The knock again, then a voice:

"Ben?"

It sounded like Inez.

"Coming."

The seventh-floor apartment was fifty bucks a week, furnished, which meant a hard bed with a history and springs that whined when you turned over; yellow curtains with plastic linings that smelled of cigarettes; a carpet into which a sort of hopelessness had settled, like dust; and a sign on the door reading: LOCK THE DOOR BEFORE YOU SLEEP.

As if I needed the reminder.

My small bedroom was connected to what the brochures had called the "living area" by a short hallway that contained a water closet. By "living area," they meant a used couch, a hot plate, and bare bulbs that flickered in the endless cycling of uneven electricity. The door leading out to the stairs was on the left as I walked from the bedroom. I stared through the peephole: a fish-eye view of Inez. She was the night clerk in the lobby bar.

"Who's it?"

"Call for you, Señor Ben."

I unlocked the door. "Is Max all right?"

"Is not your son."

"My wife?"

"Not your wife, Señor Ben. Is work. You coming?"

"I need to get dressed." I was wearing boxers that weren't so white anymore. I slipped on an undershirt and stepped into the pants on the floor and pulled suspenders with a snap over my shoulders. Then I checked my face in the mirror that hung, framed like a photograph, to the left of the door: the shock of black hair, the pale skin, the bleary eyes and bluish stubble.

The broken clock on the elbow of wall between the couch and kitchenette read 2:15.

It was always 2:15.

There was cold coffee on the hot plate from the night before, so I poured it into a cup with the ring around the rim. Housekeeping wasn't my strong point, and I don't like cold coffee. But it helped me avoid smoking, which for me was like trying to fly.

I knew the packet of Kents sat in the wastebasket under the sink. I had tossed it there the night before. I grabbed it, along with the half-eaten sandwich I now figured I might need. Today was supposed to be Day One of my new smokeless life, but I told myself that Kents got rid of the tar.

Tar is what kills you.

. . .

The phone sat on the desk in the dimly lit bar you reached through the double doors off the fading lobby. The bar served as both the Savoy's unofficial reception area and, well, the bar. It had ripped black leather cushions on metal stools, plastic napkin holders, and pressed-tin walls. The red lightbulbs made the place look like a Holland whorehouse.

Behind the bar, Inez answered the phone and sold cigarette packs with tickets slipped inside. You collected enough, you could buy a toaster. She had tacked pictures of actors she admired up and down the walls: the wrestler El Santo, Cantinflas, and Dolores del Rio, whose name meant (she said) "Sadness of the River."

She handed me the phone.

"Ben here." I slipped the cigarette into my mouth.

"Fitz." It was the department administrator, Seldon. "It's nuts over here. We need you."

"Time is it?"

"Five. Need you down here."

"The office?"

"Brentwood. One-two-three-oh-five Fifth Helena Drive."

"Come again?"

He gave me the address. I wrote it down.

"Someone died," he said.

"No kidding."

"Someone famous."

He told me who it was. I remembered reading scandal-sheet stuff about a film she hadn't finished. I had the copy of *Life* magazine with her last interview: "It might be kind of a relief to be finished," she had said. "It's sort of like, I don't know, some kind of yard dash you're running, but then you're at the finish line and you sort of sigh—you've made it! But you never have—you have to start all over again."

"Think it's maybe a . . . no, Billy," Seldon said. "Daddy's okay. Go back to bed, okay? Sorry." Back into the receiver: "Family stuff. I woke the kids."

"You woke me, too."

"Need next of kin."

"I don't handle next of kin."

"You'll handle it today."

I was a deputy coroner with clerical functions, overseeing Suicide Notes and Weapons. Sounds simple, but sometimes a suicide note is written on part of the floor, a door, mirrors, whole sections of walls. You could walk through the Sheriff's Evidence Room and see doors propped against the shelves, covered with lipstick, reading: "Dear Andrew. Tell the children I loved them."

"Hurry," Seldon said.

I tried. It took ten minutes to get the Rambler started. It was a used '58 I had purchased through the classifieds. The seller had asked me to assume his contract, which I did without knowing the abuse it had taken. It was like a battered wife that way; it ran like one, too.

I patted my pockets for a match.

Tomorrow would be Day One.

The green wooden gate outside the house sat in the middle of a stucco wall covered with bougainvilleas. It hid the property from the street, though I could see the Spanish tiles on the roof of the garage. No name on the mailbox. It was modest enough. I wondered why she'd bought it. The most famous woman in the world, with all the money that implies, but instead of a mansion in the Hills, she'd bought a one-floor hacienda in Brentwood.

This one-floor hacienda in Brentwood.

I parked in the cul-de-sac on the fifth of the numbered Helenas, tossed what was left of the third Kent to the tar, and carried my briefcase through the photographers and reporters with their press credentials lodged like playing cards in hatbands. Not to mention the neighbors gathering in their tea-rose flannel housecoats.

The sun was coming up. There were low-pressure systems in Utah and Nevada, and a southerly wind: That's what the radio said. It was going to be another scorcher.

Two cops flanked the gate.

"Morning, officers. Ben Fitzgerald. Deputy coroner."

"You're already inside."

"What?"

"LACCO is already inside."

"Not true."

"Is so. Taking pictures. A woman."

"A woman? You ask for credentials?"

"No."

I flashed my credentials. "What does this say?"

"Mr. Benjamin Fitzgerald, deputy coroner, L.A. County Coroner's Office."

"Thanks," I said.

"Fun job."

"You bet."

I walked through the living room to a hallway that led into a bedroom too small for all the people inside it now—maybe fifteen square feet. I can't remember how many; they kept coming and going. Maybe five? Then six or seven. And two or three; then seven again. A man popped his head through the door and told someone named Don to come into the kitchen, and Don stopped dusting the dresser for prints and stepped on a Sinatra record.

There were bags and boxes from I. Magnin's and Bullock's on Wilshire all over the floor. Leicas flashed as photographers took shots that would vanish tomorrow. Cops drew lines with chalk, covering the floor with a canvas cloth. My eyes darted from the detective dusting shattered glass to the copy of *Horticulture* beneath the bed to the rubber gloves spotted with liquid and the pills embedded in carpet fibers, but all of this—and everything—stopped when I saw the actress.

She was lying facedown on the bed, clutching a phone. A sheet was pulled up to her shoulders. You could see the ash-blond hair fried from too many treatments. The cord snaked underneath her body. Her fingernails were blue. The cause of death seemed obvious: an overdose. Except—

Except the body was in the soldier's position: legs straight, head down.

"I don't have to tell you what that means, Doctor," I say.

"Yes," you say. "You do."

"Well, it looked like she had been placed."

"What?"

"Placed," I say. "People who overdose don't drift happily away. There are usually convulsions. Vomiting. They die contorted. And she was clutching the phone."

"So?"

"A person dying of a barbiturate overdose would not have died clutching a phone. She might have *answered* it. But a person dying of a barbiturate overdose would have gone limp before the convulsions began."

I walked to the bed and looked down. There was no vomitus. She looked peaceful.

On the bedside table, several vials of prescription drugs sat under a lamp covered with a handkerchief. One of the vials read San Vicente

Pharmacy: "Marilyn Monroe. Engelberg . . . 7.25.62 . . . 0.5 gms . . . at bedtime."

It's the vial that sits before us now—part of your "evidence," Doctor:

Item No. 2.

Under the table was a Mexican ceramic jug, cap askew; piles of books and papers; a jar of face cream—and an empty water glass.

Remember the glass. It becomes significant.

A voice behind me: "Helluva thing."

I turned and saw Jack Clemmons in the doorway. His face was so red it looked raw, his hair the color of diluted mustard. He was West LAPD: the watch commander on duty at the western division when the call had come in that morning.

"To what do I owe the pleasure, Fitz?"

"Here for next of kin."

"There *are* no next of kin. Only a mother down at Rockhaven."

"Never heard of Rockhaven."

"You will."

"What happened here?" I asked.

"It's a helluva thing."

The housekeeper, Eunice Murray, claimed she'd noticed a light under Marilyn's door (Jack said) when she retired around ten on the previous evening. She went to bed in her own room, adjacent to Marilyn's; they share a wall. She woke at midnight and had to go to the bathroom. The bathroom was in the Telephone Room, connected to her own bedroom, but somehow she ended up in the hall in front of Marilyn's room instead. She noticed that the light was still on under the door, which was locked from the inside. She knocked: no answer.

"So what do you think she did?" Jack asked.

"She called the police."

"Oh, no, that would be too easy, Fitz. That would be too obvious. This is Hollywood. Everyone needs a twist. She didn't call the police. She called the *psychiatrist*."

"The psychiatrist?"

"Him." He pointed to a distinguished-looking, gray-haired man who stood in a suit by the window looking ashen. "Ralph Greenson. Marilyn's shrink."

"And what did *he* do?"

When Greenson arrived at the house (Jack said) he, too, found the door locked. He went outside, looked through the window, and saw the actress lying facedown and nude on the bed under rumpled bedclothes. She looked "peculiar," he said. She wasn't moving. He broke the window with a poker from the living-room fireplace and climbed inside. She was clutching the phone. "She must have been calling for help," Greenson had said.

"Why would she call for help when the housekeeper was in the next room?" I asked.

"Beats me. The shrink told Mrs. Murray, 'We've lost her,' and called Dr. Engelberg, her physician. And Dr. Engelberg called *me* at—get this, Fitz—four thirty-five A.M."

"They waited *four* hours to call the cops?"

"Yep."

"Mind if I ask the doctor a few questions?"

"You're not investigating, Ben."

"I'm curious."

"Same old Ben." He smiled. "Be my guest."

I walked up to Greenson, introduced myself, and said, "If you don't mind me asking: Why did you wait four hours to call the cops?"

"We had to get permission from the publicity department first."

"*What* publicity department?"

"Twentieth Century-Fox. Miss Monroe was filming there."

"So what did you do while you waited?"

"Talked," Greenson said.

"For *four* hours?"

"Look, I see no reason why I should go through this again. I've been through this already. I've already spoken to the coroner's office."

"*I'm* the coroner's office."

"So is she."

"Who?"

"Her." He pointed to a woman with a camera taking pictures of the space around the bed. She was maybe thirty-five and had violet eyes with dark lashes and black hair done up in a bun. She wore a gray skinned-down Norman Norell suit and stiletto shoes. Her crimson nails matched her lips. I could see the powder on her face. She reminded me of someone.

Eventually I would see her smiling up at me from behind the edge of a martini glass, moisture glistening on her front teeth, her lipstick smeared on cocktail napkins and, later, bed linens.

But for now: She was pulling something from underneath the dead star's pillow.

It was the red leather diary.

3.

The diary was filled with yellow pages on which blue handwriting had broken all the college rules. The word MEMORIES was embossed on the cover in the same gold that edged the paper. It was a dime-a-dozen diary—available at any drugstore. I had no reason to believe that it could bring down the government, Doctor. I had no reason to believe that Marilyn had died because of it, or that others would die because of it. I had no reason to believe it would jeopardize my own life or that of my family. So you ask: If I had known, would I have just walked away? Let it destroy the actress and the girl who had found it instead of all of us?

"Who are you?" I asked her.

"Jo Carnahan. LACCO."

"That's not possible."

"Anything's possible," she said. "Didn't your mother teach you that?"

"I never knew my mother."

"Sorry to hear it. And now if you'll excuse me." She walked past me, and I grabbed her elbow, spinning her sharply around.

I caught a glint in her eye, a little hidden laugh.

Who did she remind me of?

"That red book," I said. "What is it?"

"My diary."

It wasn't. You know that, Doc.

I took it from her.

"What's the big idea?" she said.

"What's *your* big idea? Impersonating an employee from the coroner's office. I was going to say a man from the coroner's office, but—"

"I'm not a man."

"I can see that. You're a thief."

"I'm not. I'm Annie Laurie."

"Thought you said your name was Jo."

"Annie Laurie is my pen name. It's a gossip column. You don't read it?"

"No," I lied. Of *course* I read it. I'd read it for years. Everyone in Southland reads it. They're lying if they say they don't. Do *you* read it, Doc?

"No."

"I thought so."

Annie Laurie is second only to Hedda Hopper and Louella Parsons when it comes to chronicling the ins and outs and ups and downs of the rich and famous. Okay, third only to Hedda and Louella. She has a husband named Dick, a Santa Anita jockey who is always on vacation; three cats; two precocious twin children perpetually at boarding school; and a cottage on Catalina. Annie Laurie has been writing her *L.A. Mirror* column, "The Voice of Hollywood," and broadcasting her WOLA radio show, *Annie Laurie Presents*, for the better part of thirty years, but she is not—unlike Parsons and Hopper—a real person; she is a character. The writers who impersonate Annie Laurie change, but Annie herself does not.

"Don't you think it's strange?" asked Jo.

"What?"

"Well, there's a bathroom in the housekeeper's room," she said. "And the carpet in here."

"What about it?"

"See how high the pile is?"

She smiled and left the room.

Guy Hockett and his son from Westwood Village Mortuary were putting Miss Monroe's body on the gurney. Rigor mortis had set in. This wasn't what the son had expected. He hadn't expected to see the source of locked-bathroom fantasies now unmovable and cold in his own hands, her bones cracking as they wrapped leather straps around her wrists and ankles.

Leather straps as if to restrain a madwoman. As if she would just get up and walk away.

They covered her in a pale blue blanket and wheeled her from the house.

A young woman screamed in the hallway, police telling her that she needed to leave because they were sealing the place.

"Keep shooting, vultures!" she shouted as I walked out. "How would *you* feel if your best friend just died?"

It was Pat Newcomb, Miss Monroe's publicist.

In the five-page death report filed by the LAPD, the deceased was described not as the star of *Some Like It Hot* or *The Seven Year Itch*—and not as the erstwhile wife of Arthur Miller and Joe DiMaggio, the most famous woman in the world—but as a "female Caucasian, age 36, height 5.4, weight 115 pounds, blonde hair, blue eyes, and slender, medium build. Occupation: actress."

The entrance to the Telephone Room, otherwise known as the guest bedroom, was across the hall from Mrs. Murray's bedroom.

I carried the diary inside and shut the door and sat on the bed by the door that led to the pool and saw a white phone on the table. There were two phones. The cord to the other phone, pink, led through the door and down the hall to where the receiver now sat on the death bed. One number, GRanite 61890, was for close friends; the other, GRanite 24830, was for everyone else.

I opened the diary.

The Book of Secrets was written in that blue scrawl on the inside page.

I turned the pages—some torn, others covered with illegible script, still others stained with unidentifiable fluids. I was searching for anything that might lead to next of kin: a lost mother, a missing son or father, a brother in Topeka, a sister in Detroit.

The diary had been started only six months before, on February 2, 2:01 A.M.:

"I hear clicking on the line,"

it read,

That's what it sounds like—Morse code. Faint voices all around. Bars are on the windows but the night is dark and the pool should be lit but it's not on account of the remodel. A few times I heard noises like people at the window but I looked around. No one there and so now, see? Who's crazy now?!!!

This was followed by a list of questions:

1. What is it like to do your job?
2. Are you going to keep J. E. H.?
3. What is next for Cuba?

The book was full of elisions, deletions, and torn pages. I saw no information about next of kin. The only number I found was RE7-8200. Others had been erased or were illegible. RE7-8200 was not only repeated; near it Marilyn had scrawled, in ragged letters, the name "Mrs. Green."

I picked up the white phone and called.

"Hello," a woman answered.

"Mrs. Green, please?"

I heard breathing. "Excuse me?"

"I'm looking for a Mrs. Green."

"Your name, please?"

"Ben Fitzgerald. L.A. County Coroner's."

"Mr. Fitzgerald, fine," she said. "But who is Mrs. Green?"

"That's what I want to know."

"There is no Mrs. Green," she said. "I've never heard of Mrs. Green."

4.

The L.A. County Morgue is in the basement of the Hall of Justice located where North Broadway forms an overpass off Santa Ana not far from Chinatown. The coroner, the sheriff's office, the D.A., and the county jail are there. The medical examiner is on the first floor. That's where my office is. There are only a few offices, because the staff is so small: three medical examiners, four lab techs, a few coroner's aides.

They call it Pneumonia Hall.

It was just after 9 A.M. I was at my desk eating the sandwich I'd retrieved from the trash and looking out the window onto the parking lot. On the blotter in front of me sat a framed picture of Rose, Max, and me smiling on the beach at Malibu: "In happier times," the caption might have read in *Photoplay*. Pigeons perched, as they always perched, on the window ledge. Every now and then I saw them mating.

"Ben," Dr. Noguchi said at the door. He was the deputy medical examiner. His first name was Thomas.

"Yeah."

"We're almost ready."

I put my sandwich down.

. . .

The most famous woman in the world was now Coroner's Case No. 81128, her toe tagged in steel crypt 33. The crypts covered a wall in the basement where the rats were. They looked like numbered freezers. I opened 33, pulling the lever below the temperature gauge, and saw the toe tags. I wheeled the body on the stretcher to Table 1 in the windowless room, looked at the flesh on bright steel with the hose and the drainage system, the sink and the suspended scale.

A sheet was pulled up over her breasts. Her eyes were closed, her hair hanging limp as if she had just washed it.

The autopsy lasted five hours.

I won't bore you with the details, Doctor, but a few things stuck with me:

Dr. Noguchi performed the procedure. This was odd. Yes, he was the only person on staff who was a university faculty member, assistant professor of pathology at Loma Linda, but he had only recently been appointed deputy medical examiner. Normally the chief medical examiner would have done it. Even stranger, Chief Coroner Curphey himself attended the autopsy, along with District Attorney John Miner.

This never happened.

"There are no puncture marks," Dr. Noguchi said into his mic as he began the external examination, and "no indication" that Monroe had injected herself. There was no indication that anyone else had injected her, either. "There's bruising," he said, "a slight ecchymotic area . . . in the left hip and left side of the lower back."

A bruise is a sign of violence. Its color comes from protein enzymes thrown off by white blood cells that try to contain the damage. Those enzymes change from dark purple to brown to yellow over time. The bruise on Miss Monroe's left hip was dark purple, which means it probably appeared on the night she died. But it was never explained.

Dr. Noguchi also noted "dual lividity." You ask me what this means: Livor mortis happens during the first eight hours after death. The heart mixes plasma with red blood cells. When the heart stops, the mixing ends, and the cells settle in the lower portion of the body. If the body is on its left side, the lividity—a purplish spotting—appears at the bottom of that side. If livor mortis is present on both sides, it's called "dual lividity."

In this case, we found livor mortis on both the back and posterior aspect of the arms and legs. Which would indicate one thing: The body had been moved.

Around twelve-thirty, Noguchi opened the stomach. It was the first abdominal organ he examined. In it, he found 20 ccs, about three tablespoons, of a brown liquid. But no pills were in the liquid. In fact, nothing indicated that she had swallowed anything poisonous.

In the duodenum, the first digestive tract after the stomach, there was "no evidence," Noguchi said, "of pills. No residue. No coloration."

"And no odor of pear," I said.

Noguchi turned to me: "What?"

"Never mind."

In his autopsy report, Noguchi summarized the digestive-system findings:

> The esophagus has a longitudinal folding mucosa. The stomach is almost completely empty. The volume is estimated to be no more than 20 cc. No residue of the pills is noted. A smear made from the gastric contents examined under the polarized microscope shows no refractile crystals. The mucosa shows marked congestion and submucosal petechial hemorrhage diffusely. The duodenum are also examined under the polarized microscope

> and show no refractile crystals. The remainder of the small intestine shows no gross abnormality. The colon shows marked congestion and purplish discoloration.

This is what created all the controversy, Doc. Why? I don't quite know where to begin, but for now: "marked congestion and purplish discoloration" may have meant the colon had been . . . compromised in the recent past.

Noguchi wrote: "Unembalmed blood is taken for alcohol and barbiturate examination. Liver, kidney, stomach and contents, urine and intestine are saved for further toxicological study." These contents were sent to Ralph J. Abernethy, the chief toxicologist.

They took a picture of the corpse and returned Case 81128 to crypt 33.

Noguchi's eventual verdict: "Suicide." He circled the word on the final report, adding the word "Probable."

The picture that you have, Doc—the one marked "62-609 8-5-62" in the evidence folder—was taken afterward. The face looks sunken because the skull was cut open to remove and weigh the brain. You have other pictures there, too, of course: one taken of the body in the broom closet of Westwood Village. And photos taken by Sinatra at Cal-Neva the week before she died.

But all that will come soon enough. At the time, I figured the whole sad business was finished, but it wasn't. It was never finished. When I returned to my office, the WHILE YOU WERE OUT slip on my desk read: "See me."

That meant only one thing.

It meant Curphey.

5.

Chief Coroner Theodore Joscelyn Curphey had a golf set in his office. It was one of those sets with a square of fake grass and a metal circle with flaps surrounding a hole you hit the ball into. He was teeing off beside his desk when I stepped inside.

"You wanted to see me?"

"One second." He hit the ball. And missed. "There." He wiped both hands together, propping the nine iron against his desk and sitting down.

His office windows, like mine, overlooked the parking lot. They were bracketed by bookshelves. A TV sat on the cabinet to the left: A roller derby show was on. A box of Dependable kitchen matches sat on the desk near the wire-webbed ashtray that held his pipe. He picked up the pipe, reignited it, and leaned back in his chair. "Have a seat," he said.

You want to know about Theodore J. Curphey, Doctor. Well, he was bald with liver spots. He had glasses with thick lenses that made his eyes pop and a mustache that made him look, more than anything, like a—

"I don't care what he looked like."

" 'Like a walrus,' I was going to say."

"He was from New York," you say. "How did he end up in L.A.?"

Northwest Airlines Flight 823 was scheduled to depart LaGuardia for Miami at 2:45 P.M. on February 1, 1957, but takeoff was delayed for three hours on account of the snow. There was a *lot* of snow. Despite a slight sliding of the nosewheel on pavement, the flight was cleared around 6 P.M. There was a normal roll, the first stage of takeoff, but the DC-6A did not achieve sufficient altitude over Flushing Bay, and sixty seconds after it became airborne, the craft clipped the treetops over Rikers Island.

It crashed.

Twenty people died.

Curphey's work on the case brought him to the attention of Los Angeles County. Later that year, he became the county's first coroner. There was resentment at the morgue: An outsider—from New York, no less—was now boss. Some think that's how he got into trouble: A rat went to Bonelli and the Board of Supervisors with information about the tissue samples kept in the storage room on Kohler.

But more on that later.

"Siddown, Ben."

I did.

He looked at me over those thick glasses. "I just wanted to check in," Curphey said. "See how you're doing."

"Okay, I think."

He opened the personnel file on his desk and paged through its papers, reading. At one point he frowned and looked up at me, squinting. "Thirty-three years old."

"Yes."

"A Step Three."

"Yes."

"Good-looking young man."

"Thank you."

"You started with us as . . ."

"Deputy coroner, Suicide Notes and Weapons. I was an embalmer before."

"So you wanted a change."

"The truth is I wanted more money. My son was born. I needed it. So I took the civil service exam and the walk-through test."

"The walk-through test?"

"You have to walk through this place and not pass out."

He did not find this funny. He returned to the papers, shuffling through them until he looked up, adjusted his glasses, and said, "Well, we certainly appreciate the work you do, Ben. Not to mention what you did for us at trial."

"Of course."

"Another man, a lesser man, might have balked."

"All right." Where was he going with this?

"I'm curious to hear your thoughts on what happened today."

"I don't know what you mean."

"During the autopsy. What's your verdict?"

"It's not my place to say."

"It wasn't your place to say that there was no odor of pear, either, but you said it. Why?"

"A chloral overdose always smells of pear, and there were no refractile crystals and no—"

"The tox report will tell us everything we need to know."

"She was in the soldier's position when we found her, sir. She was clutching the phone. A person dying of a barbiturate overdose would not have died clutching a phone."

"So," he said, "is *that* why you called the Justice Department?"

"I'm sorry?"

"I got a call from a friend at the Justice Department in Washington, and he said that at eight-oh-nine A.M., precisely, a woman named Angie Novello received a phone call from one . . . Ben Fitzgerald at the L.A. County Morgue. It originated from the Monroe house. He said this Ben was looking for a 'Mrs. Green.'" Curphey took his glasses off and stared at me. "Why did you call the Justice Department?"

"I was looking for next of kin."

"At the *Justice* Department?"

"It was a number I had."

"A number."

"I found it in a notebook. At the Monroe house."

"What type of notebook?"

"Seemed to be a diary."

"What was in the diary?"

"I don't know. I didn't read it."

"Where is it now?"

"I left it back at the house."

"Let me make something clear, Ben." He leaned forward. "It's not your job to speculate."

"You asked my opinion."

"You're not coroner yet."

"I play golf as well as anyone."

"I don't want you making any more phone calls."

"What about next of kin?"

"The next-of-kin bullshit is just bullshit, a formality. Everyone knows the girl's mother is out at Rockhaven. If you want next of kin, that's who you want to see. Go visit her. Tell her what happened to her poor dead daughter, if she doesn't know already, and you've done your job."

"Yes, sir."

"Are we clear?"

"Crystal."

But I knew what I had to do. And to do it I needed a flashlight.

6.

The flashlight was cheap, but that was okay. I didn't need a good one. I paid for it at True Value and put it on the shotgun seat, took Temple to Wilshire and San Vicente back down to the numbered Helenas and the Brentwood hacienda.

"Relative humidity is sixty-two percent," said the man on the Rambler radio. "The temperature humidity index stands at seventy-three, and the wind is calm. Marilyn Monroe is dead, apparently from an overdose of sleeping pills. An investigation is ongoing, but here is the statement from Deputy Coroner Cronkite . . ."

The day was ending, the lights in the basin below the spray of palms spreading out like fire in a grid under the sky. There was a moon. You could see the smaller lights from cars along the highway winding like a silver river through the trees.

I parked past the scalloped gate in the wall on Fifth.

Now you ask why I returned, because I care about my job, but there are opportunities in life for gaining knowledge and experience, Doc, and I couldn't stop thinking of that little red memory book. It seemed to contain the solution to a mystery. All right, *and* I was covering my ass. Curphey knew something. He knew that people who overdose on chloral smell of pear; he knew that anyone with all those Nembutals in her stomach would have been yellow inside. He knew what it meant that we'd found no refractile crystals. But he didn't like that *I* knew—or had noticed—all this. He was playing some kind of a game, and I didn't want to get screwed the way that I'd been screwed before.

So go back through the microfilm, Doc, and in January you will see images of me testifying at the hearings, along with the headline:

ACCUSED OF WILLFUL MISUSE OF OFFICE!

Curphey was charged with nine counts involving the removal of organ tissue from bodies during postmortem examinations in cases that involved accidents or "mystery deaths." That's what the paper called them. He had asked for the tissue to be removed even when the organs were not involved with the cause of death; the relatives of the deceased were never told how their dear ones were mutilated.

County Board of Supervisors chairman Frank G. Bonelli testified that his office received more complaints about the coroner's department than any other agency, and Supervisor Hahn called for an explanation of "pig pen" conditions in the LACCO storage room at 754 Kohler.

I knew that storage room; I had taken the tissue samples there, but that's not what I told the jury.

After we won, we all went out to celebrate on the county's dime, which led to the images that you have surely seen, Doctor. You've heard of the *L.A. Mirror*?

"Of course."

"My wife, of all people, believed what they wrote. Which is why she kicked me out—"

"Stick to the point," you say.

Okay: The cul-de-sac was dark.

A cop stood outside the gate, a kid puffing out his chest like a bird.

"Evening," I said.

"Evening, sir."

"Need to get inside."

"There's a sign on the door. Says 'Any person breaking into or entering these premises will be prosecuted to the fullest extent of the law.'"

I showed him my badge. "LACCO."

"I can read. I am under orders not to let in anyone else from the coroner's office."

"I work for Curphey."

"Orders from Curphey: no one inside."

"Look, I'm in a bit of trouble—"

"Buddy. Read my lips, okay. Get the fuck out of here."

"I just hoped that—"

"What part of 'get the fuck out of here' don't you understand?"

"The 'fuck' part," I said. "I flunked biology."

He reached for his gun.

"All right." I raised my hands and backed up. "Don't get all Gary Cooper on me."

I put the car in reverse, right arm around the passenger seat as if it were a girl, and looked back through the window. I was careful not to clip the cars parked on both sides of the street as I pulled into a dark driveway, then took a right out of Fifth.

On Carmelina, I parked and sat and thought and needed to stop thinking. I got in trouble when I thought, but then so did Galileo. Not to mention Jack Paar.

I got out of the car.

There were no streetlights, so I walked under the dark jacarandas down Sixth to another cul-de-sac. There was a locked gate to the right. It fronted on a driveway. I vaulted over it, walked along the strip of land between the driveway and another house, and through the backyard all the way to Miss Monroe's pool.

I took a left and walked along the narrow lawn to the window of the room where she had died. The glass had already been broken the night before, so I pulled myself up and dropped down inside.

And here the tape breaks. It's at 12583. "Fuck," you say, and stub your Chesterfield, trying to splice it together. Then you feed it back through the reels and hit RECORD.

"So you climbed inside."

"I found the diary where I'd left it, Doctor, under the pillow in the Telephone Room, and when I picked it up I remembered what Jo had said about the bathroom and the carpet."

"What about it?" you ask.

"Well, she'd said there was a bathroom in the housekeeper's room and mentioned the height of the carpet pile. And suddenly I knew what all this meant."

"What did it mean?"

I went into Eunice Murray's room and flipped the switch, but the power had already been shut off. I shone the flashlight around. The room was neat, orderly, the same layout as Marilyn's, the bed against the left wall. On the opposite side of the bed, near the window overlooking the pool, a door on the left led into a bathroom that connected to the Telephone Room.

So let's get this straight, Doctor: Mrs. Murray said she'd woken up because she needed to use the bathroom. That (she claimed) was how and why she'd seen the light under Marilyn's door. But why would she have gone into the hall when her bathroom was accessible through her own room?

Then I went inside Marilyn's room. I put the flashlight on the floor facing the hall and closed the door. The carpet pile was so high that it scraped against the underside of the door when I closed it.

The carpet hid the light.

"I don't think this adds up to much," you say.

"I think it adds up to a lot."

There are logical problems with Mrs. Murray's testimony, Doctor; there was a four-hour gap between the time the docs arrived and the call to the police. We found no yellow color in the digestive tract, and no refractile crystals: no evidence that Marilyn had *ingested* pills. The body showed dual lividity, which indicates that it was moved.

"So?" you say.

"*Why* was the body moved?"

"Let's stick to the subject at hand," you say. "You found the diary in the Telephone Room. Did you read it?"

"Yes."

I sat on the deathbed. The flashlight illuminated MEMORIES on the cover. I felt the red leather, saw gold on the edge.

And opened it.

THE BOOK OF SECRETS

7.

February 2, 2:01 a.m. I hear clicking on the line. That's what it sounds like—Morse code. Faint voices all around. Bars are on the windows but the night is dark and the pool should be lit but it's not on account of the remodel. A few times I heard noises like people at the window but I looked around. No one there and so now, see? Who's crazy now?!!!

Mrs. Murray is padding around in her slippers I can hear her padding through the door and once I thought about getting up and going to talk but don't feel like it. I called a few people. NO ONE was home, or they were all ignoring me. They *always* ignore me so all I have left is YOU, Diary!!

They are following me I know it there are wires in the walls I have called Fred and there are bugs. I don't mean insects.

Tonight I went to dinner at the beach house and Danny helped me with the notes. I still have them in my purse:

1. What is it like to do your job?
2. Are you going to keep J. E. H.?
3. What is next for Cuba?

I was late I am always late so they expected it. We drove to where the highway is Beach Road under the bluffs and went down the hill through the gate into the room and they were eating dinner at the table when I walked in. Some of them, like the surfers Pat hates, were barefoot.

Peter said, "Drink?"

I was already drunk but "yes" I took the glass and everyone said hi and Peter introduced me to the General.

The chair to the left of the General was empty and that was my plate. I mean the one that was untouched and napkins and silverware beside it and the glass near the candelabras where a Polaroid camera sat and it was new. They were taking pictures.

"Nice to meet you." I hardly looked at the General. I sat and pretended that I didn't care and wasn't impressed. He pretended the same, dear Diary.

Diary, I had another glass and the room got warm and I giggled at a joke someone had made. I wasn't looking at the General and wondered if he was laughing.

Then I turned to him.

The General was looking across the table at Peter, his mouth smiling but his eyes were not and saw me staring at him and I think his smile died. He looked serious. Well, Diary, lust is more serious than anything.

He kept staring. I kept the glass against my lips. It became a Point that I was making with that lipstick, a Thing I did like ice on nipples. It drove men MAD!!!! Well, just press a glass to lips and let the color bleed on crystal and keep it there and see what happens.

It happened to him. Well, that Adam's apple bobbed and he reached under the table and touched my thigh it sparked with the static from the helicopter that landed behind the house and you *know* the neighbors just hated the sand in their pool!!!!

I jumped and champagne spilled and he took his hand away and "Oh gosh sorry let me" and wiped my dress with his napkin and realized what he was doing and looked up with Peter pouring more champagne, his sister laughing though angry at the surfers and all that damn sand from bare feet and dropped the napkin he was shrugging like the awkward altar boy you *know* he was, Diary!!!!

I turned to the General.

"What," I said, "is next for Cuba?"

Down the long line of the beach I could see the lights of the Pier and the farther pier in the fog off the ocean, the Ferris and merry-go-round where I'd once stood watching couples on the tilting chairs. Well, I'd eaten cotton candy and worn the wig and wandered the city to buy a wedding ring. Well, the salespeople were rude. They didn't know who I was. I had a black wig on and they didn't care.

Sometimes I don't think straight.

"I didn't want to say it back in the house," the General said. I could hardly hear over the waves. You could hear sounds on the highway and music drifted over the waves. You can hear things that way. I know that!!! (Even voices.) "You just have to stop calling," he said.

"He calls *me* when he needs to."

"That's different. He has different needs."

"How different than *mine*?"

"He's a busy man."

"*I'm* busy, too, for fuck's sake. You think I'm not? But I know what matters in life. I make time for other people."

"Tell that to your mother."

"Oh, now that was a low. That was really a low—"

"I'm sorry. Look—"

"He *gave* me his number. He said I could call. And suddenly it doesn't work. So I have to call the fucking switchboard?"

"You have so many people," he said. "There must be thousands."

It wasn't true. Everybody thinks the phone rings all the time but men don't have the nerve to call, not the right ones. And once in a while I meet a nice guy and I know it's going to work. He doesn't have to be from Hollywood he doesn't have to be an actor. And we have a few drinks and go to bed. Then I see his eyes glaze over and I can see it going through his mind: "Oh my God I'm going to fuck Marilyn Monroe" and he can't get it up.

"I understand," the General said. "But you have to stop calling him. From now on, why don't you try calling *me*?"

He took my hand and I felt sparks more than static and looked at him and was it a truly kind face in the light from the houses? The houses were along the bluffs and the children that I always watched played around the nets but it was dark where we stood so I couldn't *really* see him. So was it kindness or just the reflection of something?

"I hear you have a new house," he said. "Will you let me see your house?"

I don't remember how I answered I don't remember now and the clock by my bed reads 3:15. The minute hand keeps moving. I wish it would stop, Diary!

I have taken another couple from the vial by the bed and there are six. I wrote the number that I started with down and it was eight. You see it written here I always write it I started with eight so I want to be sure. They say that I am special and I'm wondering if the moment is coming when I will close my eyes and the things that seem real bleed into what can't be. That's the second you know you are slipping which is what I feel now a slow slipping. I can't finish the conversation I want to write it out, what I remember, but am falling asleep leap a leap and so I won't forget:

8.

The flashlight bobbed on those last scrawled lines, but I turned its dying circle to the door when I heard the noise. There were sirens in the distance and rain in the jacarandas, but what I *really* heard was inside. A tumbler click? A key turning in a lock? I stood, the beam fading. The flashlight was cheap. I've said that already. I switched it off and walked to the door that led into the hall.

I looked out.

A noise: something in the living room, the low sweep of light.

A silhouette stepped into the hall, raising his own flashlight toward me as I jumped back inside Marilyn's room and pressed myself against the wall behind the door, eyeing the broken window and listening as the men—there were two now—entered the Telephone Room:

"—red," the voice said.

"So much shit." Another voice. "Who knew she had it?"

"Nothing here."

"You *what*?"

"I said there's nothing. I said there's . . . I don't see it."

"Let's look in the other room. Maybe they got it wrong."

"The captain said—"

"Come on."

"He would have to—"

"It's not in here. Nothing's in here."

"Except a bunch of shit. Let's try the other room."

I pressed myself against the wall behind the door, hands flat on both sides, my face all eyes.

The beam swept the room.

I held my breath.

The beam steadied on the bed, landing on the diary.

"There it is!"

I ran and grabbed the diary from the bed and darted to the broken window, cutting myself on the glass left in the frame, and dropped to the lawn.

"Grab his jacket!"

I heard crickets and barking dogs in the air out on Sixth. I thought of Mrs. Murray's testimony, Miss Monroe in the soldier's position, no refractile crystals, the missing yellow, the entry in the diary—

I jumped over the fence and ran to the cul-de-sac.

A van marked B. F. FOX ELECTRIC was parked down the street from my car. It hadn't been there before.

I got inside the Rambler. The engine wouldn't turn. I sat turning the key, lights and radio flashing, then dying as the cheap bastard sparked out.

I pushed the diary onto the floor, kicked it under the seats as the engine clicked and I drove straight into the man. I couldn't see his face. He fell to the street, picking himself up just as I turned and sped down Sixth.

In the rearview mirror, I saw them coming.

It was 8:01. And I was late.

9.

"You're late," Rose said as she took a blackened casserole from the oven and put it on the counter to the right of the sink. She wore an apron and mitts. She opened the lid, waving away smoke with those Mickey Mouse hands. "Burned," she said, and turned to me. "You were supposed to pick him up an hour ago."

"I got delayed at work."

"Sure, it's always work. Don't tell me."

"It's something this time."

"Like . . . what? The tissue samples?"

"Hey."

"I'm sorry." She shook her head. "I didn't mean it."

We were in El Segundo, not far from the airport. The name means "the second" in Spanish, since it's only the second location in the U.S. to host a Standard Oil plant.

That tells you almost everything you need to know.

The house was where I'd lived until just after the trial, the place where we had tried to make a home. Rose sighed, deflated, and shrugged with a slap of both mitts against her summer dress. She had long brown hair that she was always brushing behind her ears and skin that looked like a soap commercial. She smelled of soap, too.

Someone once asked, "What is there to say about love that someone else hasn't already made money off of?" I don't have an answer to that. I don't have anything to say about love. I certainly never made money off it. Rose once cut my black hair with clippers in the kitchen and, picking it up from the floor, said, "Too bad I can't sell this."

She had fallen in love, she said, with my hair and the way it curled around my ears and the way one ear stuck out more than the other and the way my eyebrows looked, she said. That and, she said, my hands. For me it was the same. It's the details that you notice—the slight damp on the back of her neck, the way she clips her fingernails.

Now I held *The Book of Secrets* up to her. "The diary," I said. "Of Marilyn Monroe."

"Well, that's just great, but how does that put food on the table?"

"There's food on the table."

"The damn cookbook doesn't work. It's like that sweater you gave me."

"Which?"

"The one that never kept me warm. We'll have to get dinner out."

"I don't mind."

"I don't mean *you*," she said. "Someone's coming over."

"What kind of someone?"

"We've discussed this before: It's a trial separation."

"When do we reach a verdict?"

"We already did. You can only make so many withdrawals from an emotional bank account before it's empty."

"Are you seeing that therapist again?"

"I need to stand up for myself."

"You're seeing that therapist again."

"I need to take care of Max."

"You *do* take care of him."

"You know what he asked me last night?"

"No."

"He wanted to know what a whore was. Some kid told Max that his father was caught with a whore and there are pictures to prove it. So Max—"

"I wasn't caught with a whore."

"That's not what the *Mirror* said. I want to show you something." She walked from the kitchen through the dining room to the living room where Max sat playing Monopoly on the carpet.

I followed.

"Max?"

My son looked up, and I don't know how to tell you what I felt about him, Doc. He was nine. He was four feet and four inches. He was the most beautiful kid in the world. You wouldn't believe *how* beautiful.

And there he sat. I see him now: playing with the game he didn't know how to play, using the silver pieces as toys.

His favorite was the thimble.

"Show Ben what's on your leg."

It was "Ben": not "Dad" or "Daddy."

"Do I haf to?"

"Yes," she said as the boy stood and shambled over to where I stood. He sheepishly slipped from the beige corduroys he wore with the gray T-shirt. He wore Batman underwear. Rose pointed to the tiny marks in a small, symmetrical cluster near his ankle.

"Look at this, Ben," she said. "Do you know what this is?"

"Bites."

"Bedbugs. From your fleabag hotel."

"It's not a hotel."

"The hotel where he spends every other week. God only

knows what else he's getting from that place. VD from the toilet seats—"

I cupped my hands over Max's ears. They were small and warm. "Little pitchers. My apartment is fine, Rose."

"Your *hotel*—"

"Please," I said. "Let's go into the bedroom."

The bedroom was in disarray: clothes on the floor, the bed unmade, the picture of Rose, Max, and me that had sat by the alarm clock on the bedside table turned to the wall. Moving boxes sat around the bed, filled with my stuff: books, the old model train I had bought for Max's last birthday and assembled in the basement, my typewriter, a stack of jazz albums Rose had never liked, a few 8mm W. C. Fields movies, and a baseball bat.

"We need to make this fast," she said. "I want custody of Max."

Like a punch in the gut. "You're kidding me?"

"—lieved," she said over the plane flying low into the airport.

"You what?"

"I said I thought you'd be relieved."

"To lose my son?"

"To have more time. To kiss Daddy Curphey's ass."

"I don't kiss ass."

"You perjured yourself."

"I got a promotion."

"Step Three? That's what you got in return for your soul? Faust at least got Gretchen. *You* got a bottle of bourbon in a Wilshire hotel."

"It's not a hotel. It's the Savoy."

"On *Wilshire*."

"I think I should remind you that you kicked me out."

"You want me to remind you why?"

"The *Mirror* lied," I said.

"Oh, and *you* chopped down the cherry tree."

The doorbell rang. "Jesus," she said.

10.

I suppose that I can trace the death of my marriage to the afternoon we won the lawsuit, Doc, after which we all repaired to a place called Verona Gardens. It had once been a tony nightclub—it was now a hotel—on Hollywood Boulevard.

We started with some fancy drinks that seemingly shielded us from excess through egg whites and umbrellas, but it wasn't long before we achieved a kind of liftoff on the harder stuff, and the next thing I knew we were drinking shots straight from someone's bottle.

Everyone was toasting me. My testimony had made me a hero, the new deputy coroner, Step Three, and with every shot I felt that I was taking yet another step away from my own past. I was a big man, important, and had proved it in the courthouse. I wasn't going to end up lost, a failure out in San Berdoo, hulling beans.

This is what I kept telling the woman who had, like everything else, lurched out of nowhere. She liked my hair, she said. She kept touching it, telling me that it was black and not only black but glossy and beautiful and how my lips were red against the white of the skin and the bluish stubble of beard. "You Irish?" she asked.

"Black Irish."

"Black," she said, "is sexy, freaky."

The next thing I knew I woke on a bed that was smeared with blood. An ashtray filled with butts sat in the sun that streamed through open blinds. There were bowls of half-eaten Chinese food. Some of it was dripping on the walls.

The phone was ringing.

"Jesus."

I stood, still in my clothes, and stumbled to the phone, trying to piece together the story of the night from the evidence of things around me.

Lipstick on the mirror read, "So long, sucker."

She had emptied out my wallet.

"Hello?" I said.

"This Ben Fitzgerald?"

"Yes," I said. "Who's—"

"Duane Mikkelson. From the *Mirror.* You heard of it?"

Is this my boy?" Rose's New Friend said as he entered the house, taking his hat off and smiling down at Max, who was playing in his underwear. "This must be my boy."

Max looked up.

The New Friend bent to tickle my son's face with his forefinger. "Or is this a monkey?"

The New Friend was older—forty-eight at least—with a thick gray mustache slightly twirled at the edges and gray hair so precisely parted and pomaded it looked plastic. He was Santa Claus with a shave and a haircut.

He looked like money.

He also looked like a flit.

"Rose," I said. "Let's put Max's pants on."

The New Friend looked up at me.

"Mr. Charles," my wife said, "this is Ben. Ben, this is—"

"Reginald Charles." He extended his hand. "Very pleased to meet you."

I shook his hand. "Nice to meet you, too. I'm afraid dinner is ruined. The cookbook didn't work."

"Oh, a shame."

"Neither did the sweater," I said.

"What?"

"Never mind."

"Ben was just leaving," Rose said.

I brought Max's pants to the boy and held them out for him to step in. "Come on, buddy. We're going to the park."

"You're not taking him to Pacific Ocean, are you?" Rose asked.

"Sure am."

"Yay!" Max said.

"That place is a death trap," said Rose.

"At least there are no bedbugs."

11.

A drinker loses time. I knew this from my dad. A drinker's life disappears, like magic, from 5 P.M. to 3 A.M. To recapture the hours, he must be a daily detective of his own ashtrays and bar food, his napkins and the lipstick on unfiltered Pall Malls, his stained sheets and the smell of hops under the streetlight in the back of the bar where the fans kick out exhaust. He must be a detective of his own soggy evenings, as I had been the morning after the trial—or as I was when, that night, I found myself in a part of town I didn't know.

"This is Titusville Air," the friendly voice said on the radio.

The reception started going out when the lights from the only other car on the road rose in the rearview.

It was a Ford Fairlane. Dice dangled from the rearview mirror. It tailed me for maybe five miles but disappeared when I finally found the PCH and, soon afterward, Pacific Ocean Park.

"Dad?" Max asked in the shotgun seat.

"Yeah."

"What do you get when you cross an elephant and a rhinoceros?"

"I give up, Max. What?"

"Hell-if-I-know."

"That's a good one, sport. That's really a good one."

The park stretched across a three-block swath of Venice, like a *T* with its stem jutting into the ocean. At the tip was an island overlooking the Pacific; you reached it only on the Ocean Skyway bubble carts. I parked in the Ocean lot in a part of town you know is rundown. Venice. You've been there. Rose thought it was a "death trap" and "dangerous and unsanitary," just like the Savoy.

It wasn't. But a man whose wife is divorcing him has only a few options, one of which involves giving the son those things that she denies. These "things," she now claims, included Wild Turkey and pills, which is a lie. You know that, Doctor.

"I don't," you say.

I grabbed the diary and held my son's hand as we left the car and walked past the lights around the fountains with the dolphins and the swirling Neptune and the starfish at the top of the rotating pole to the ticket window under yellow arches. Behind the Plexiglas, in the green fluorescent light, sat a woman whose head barely cleared the low shelf.

"Two, please."

"One ninety-eight."

We walked into the park that stretched down to the island at the end with the sound of laughing and the *ca-ching* of clown heads ejecting at the pop of water rifles and the lights of the city in the sky over the Santa Monicas. Yellow and green neon lit the balls above the hot dog and the cotton candy stands.

"Where to, sport?"

"Around the World in Eighty Turns."

"You always get sick on that one."

"*Mom* gets sick on that one."

"Okay." I wondered how far I should go. "How *is* she, sport?"

"She's okay. She's seeing people."

"People."

"Like the man. She put an ad in."

"Where?"

"Newspaper. For testing boyfriends."

"What kind?"

"Other daddies, I guess. She's mad at you," he said. "But I can help."

"How?"

"Here." He took the Get Out of Jail Free card from his pocket. "It's the only one I have."

I bent down, hands on his small shoulders, and looked straight into his face. "You know something?" I said. "I'm gonna keep this forever."

And I will.

Later, he threw up in the toilet of the Savoy because his belly hurt, he said, thanks to Around the World in 80 Turns, a trip we'd taken twice, and while I sat on the edge of the bed, hand on his damp forehead, I heard the rattling in his chest. He was clutching his silver thimble.

He was having an asthma attack, Doctor. He has asthma. So, at 2:15, I took him for a drive. It's pretty much the only cure. You roll the windows down. You try to clear his lungs.

We drove for hours.

At 2:15, we returned to the hotel and I carried my sleeping son up the stairs to the room on the seventh floor. I sat watching his chest rise and fall behind his T-shirt as the lights elongated on the ceiling from the cars on Wilshire. Some dwindled into nothing as they passed.

Some didn't.

When he finally slept, I reached for the Wild Turkey in the kitchen cupboard, took the Kent pack from my pocket, and carried *The Book of Secrets* to the sofa that faced the window over Wilshire.

I opened it and read.

The tape moves slowly. You stare at me, eyes wide, the cigarette burning all the way down to your fingers.

"So," you finally ask. "What did you read?"

"Tell me where Max is first."

"I don't have to tell you anything."

"Talk about a double standard."

"You're under arrest. How many times do I need to remind you of that? Now, what was in the diary?"

I say nothing.

The tape is at 23462.

You take a long drag, cupping your hand over your mouth, and squint against the smoke. "I will wait for five more minutes."

The tape: 23465, 23466, 23467.

"Time's up." You stand, turn the Sony off, carrying all but one unused tape from the room. The door slams with the deep echo of metal. The keys hanging from the ring around your belt jangle as, no doubt, you lock the door.

Seconds later, the lock clicks again. The guard enters, pasty face and dull eyes, and clears away the evidence:

1. The Smith & Wesson
2. A vial of Nembutal
3. A piece of notebook paper reading "Chalet 52" and "July 28"
4. A stained manila folder containing a number of 8 × 10 photographs

5. *Amahl and the Night Visitors*
6. A bag of ashes
7. A new red MEMORIES diary

The guard looks briefly up at me but doesn't say a thing. He leaves the room and locks the door.

I hear ticking, footsteps, and then nothing else for hours.

12.

It's hard to tell how much time has passed. There are no windows in the room with the green paint and the ceiling with the light and the fan. I stare at the recorder that is the only thing left—that and the ashtray filled with spent cigarettes but no lighter or matches. It sits on a folded newspaper, dated October 22:

"Let's be clear-headed on Communism!" an ad reads. "The League strongly supports the President's over-due decision to act against the Soviet build-up in Cuba."

I sleep, briefly, but I see what I always see when I close my eyes: the drugged woman, crouched on all fours.

They never turn the light out.

The Novril is wearing off. I don't know what time it is—there is no clock—but hours must have passed and the ache is everywhere. I suppose that is why my voice is hard to understand when I finally thread the unused tape into the Sony, clear my throat, and press RECORD:

"Okay" (I say). "I'll tell you. The entry I read in the diary was about sex. The man she met at the party, the one she called the General, who wanted to see her house? He showed up at the house. And she showed her house to him. They had sex. Because she believed his lies, just like she believed his brother's. He wore dirty white socks, okay?"

Then I shout: "Isn't this what you wanted?"

No one responds, so I shout until I am hoarse:

"She said he wore white socks under his suit! Said he was like a little boy! He came to see her house the morning after the party! They ended up in bed! He ended up—"

The door opens. You walk in with a plate of food and—thank you, sir—the vial of Novril.

I reach for it.

"Grabby! Hang on, now. Eat first. A boy's got to keep his strength up." You pick the chicken off the bone in mealy shreds and hold it to my lips, feeding me; when I am finished, you say, "Dessert."

Dessert is three Novrils.

I suck the bitter pills from your fingers; the pain fades, my vision blurs, and the whoosh from the vent on the floor is all I can hear as you adjust your glasses and ask one question. Then another.

—try to say that I can't hear you, but you don't understand. It's silent except for the sea in my head, the sound from the air vent below.

13.

February 2, 11:05 p.m. The funny thing was the socks they were white. He wasn't like the Commander he was a boy and gosh so sloppy. He came to see my house. "I hear you have a new house. Will you let me see your house?" But that is like the joke about the etchings he wanted to come up and see them but it was more because it always is.

"Hi," he said at the door. He had a bottle of Dom Pérignon. It's what I like and Peter must have told him. "House-warming present," he said.

I think the word is *sheepish*.

I said thank you and tried to get him to relax because he didn't so I put the champagne on ice and was thinking maybe we might drink it later.

I am drinking it now.

But I was nervous, too, Diary!!!! And why torture yourself with hellos? Well, I showed him the house it wasn't finished on account of I'd just moved. Well, he knew that. The red couch was delivered to the cottage and everything needed fixing but "here is the living room. The couch will go there. It's Norman Norell. The furniture came from Mexico, a lot of it. Taxco. Eunice helped. The fireplace works. Kiva. I haven't lit it yet."

I took him through the hall that led from the living room into the Telephone Room, Mrs. Murray's room and my room.

My room is where I am now drinking and writing and wondering if this will make sense.

The windows are covered with shades they call them black-outs I can't sleep if the sun or moon comes inside but the reason I want the shades is so that I don't see the Man.

He is there now.

I take a Nembutal and wash it down with his Dom. The yellow is so pretty and pretty soon I take another with the champagne open on the floor and once I knocked the bottle over or maybe someone else did.

Okay, get to the point. I am sorry, diary, but the point is that the sheets are still dirty and smell of him or should I say his socks? The stain is on the sheets and then inside me.

"This is the bedroom," I said and he just stared kind of gulping like he was swallowing, that Adam's apple bob. He was shorter than me so I tried bending down but it didn't really work.

"Well," he said. "So this is it."

"The bedroom."

"This is the bedroom."

I was thinking it might happen with the champagne later but it happened then when he leaned to kiss me first my cheek and then he was all over me "like," as they say, "a cheap suit." Well the suit wasn't cheap but he wore socks under the trousers. NEWS FLASH!!!! *White* socks.

I said that already.

Then he was almost naked in his underwear and white socks I

kept laughing at the socks and when I pulled on the edge of his shorts I saw the wrinkly lolling thing like an ugly Florida of flesh that always made me laugh but I tried not to. It was sadder than his socks. Well you can't laugh at that.

But I couldn't help it so he needed to show me how important he was to establish his power which is why he told me what he shouldn't have. He talked about the Bay of Pigs. He talked about Castro.

I wrote it down, dear diary. I made notes on a napkin after he left:

> Robert Maheu at the Brown Derby. Johnny Roselli. Poison in a pen or Castro's soup. Or [redacted] But Jack pulled the plug. When all those boats hit *Bahia de Cochinos*, and all the rebels died. The CIA. The CIA.

That was it. That was all. I wasn't sure what it meant but I knew that this was his little-boy little-man search for approval.

From ME!!!!!

Dad?"

I jumped and dropped the diary to the floor. I turned and saw Max. He was standing at the end of the hall, rubbing his eyes with his knuckles.

"Jeez, Maxie, you scared me."

"Sorry, Dad."

"How you feeling?"

"Fine."

"The bad air gone?"

"It's gone. What are you doing up?"

"I could ask you the same question, sport. It's late."

"It's early."

It was 2:15.

"You're smoking again," he said.

"I'm not."

"You have cigarettes."

"Didn't light them."

"You were *going* to."

I picked the Kent pack up, crushed it, and dropped it to the floor. "You happy?"

He nodded.

"Now, go back to bed."

"Tuck me in again?"

"Sure."

I walked him down the hall and tucked in his toes and then pulled the bedspread up to just under his chin and kissed his forehead. "Now, you go back to sleep. How many fingers?" I asked at the door.

"Three."

I left the door open three fingers so that he could see into the hall and was heading back to the front room when I heard his voice: "Dad?"

"Yeah, sport?"

"Where's Mom?"

"Home."

"Why aren't *you* home?"

Hey, try answering that one, smart guy. "I wish I knew," I said. "Now, go to bed."

Back in the living room, I picked up my glass, saw the light in the last of the bourbon, and drained it.

I drifted into sleep, awakening either two minutes or two hours later to the sound of honking outside.

It was 2:15.

The car kept honking, someone laying on the horn.

Someone was yelling, “Shattap!”

I walked across the room and looked out.

It was the Ford Fairlane.

MONDAY, AUGUST 6

14.

MARILYN MONROE FOUND DEAD!

Sleeping pill overdose! Empty bottle near bed!

I bought the *Times* from the newsstand on the sidewalk and carried it back to 7-A and sat on the couch while Max slept. I read everything anyone knew about the death that was bigger than the Soviet explosion of a nuclear bomb in Uppsala, bigger than Nixon at the helm of the GOP, bigger than the fact that little William Webb, Jr., the state's only Thalidomide baby, would undergo a bone graft from his legs to his arms on August 23.

Russia's newspaper *Izvestia* claimed that Hollywood and "Western values" had killed Monroe.

Coroner Curphey offered his "presumptive opinion" that death was due to "an overdose of a drug. Further toxicological and microscopic studies should be available within forty-eight hours, though it will be about a week before an investigation establishes whether or not Miss Monroe's death was an accident."

But the big news came from Marshall Cantwell's article in the *Times*:

Mrs. Monroe's body was discovered after her housekeeper and companion, Mrs. Eunice Murray, awoke about 3 a.m. and saw a light still burning in the actress's room.

But the bedroom door was locked. She was unable to arouse [*sic*] Miss Monroe by shouts and rapping on the door, and immediately telephoned Miss Monroe's psychiatrist, Dr. Ralph Greenson.

Dr. Greenson took a poker from the fireplace, smashed in a window, and climbed into the Monroe bedroom. He took the telephone from her hand and told Mrs. Murray, "She appears to be dead."

He called Dr. Hyman Engelberg, who had prescribed the sleeping pills, and pronounced her dead on his arrival at the house a short time later.

Dr. Engelberg called police at 4:20 a.m. and two officers arrived in five minutes.

Do I need to tell you what's wrong with this picture, Doctor? Mrs. Murray, Dr. Greenson, and Dr. Engelberg had all told Jack Clemmons that Murray woke just after midnight. But here the time had been conveniently moved forward three hours.

In the same article, Pat Newcomb was said to be "nearly hysterical with grief" and was quoted: "When your best friend kills herself, how do you feel? What do you do?" She added: "This must have been an accident."

Her best friend killed herself. But it was an accident.

I dropped Max off at summer school in El Segundo, then headed to the Esso station. I fiddled with the radio knob until I landed on

Annie Laurie Presents. I heard swelling strings and an announcer saying, "Live from Hollywood, it's *Annie Laurie Presents*—and *this* is Annie Laurie!"

Then Jo's voice, like mink incarnate: "Hello, dear ones! 'I was never used to being happy, so that wasn't something I ever took for granted.' Now, who said those words? The answer: the late Marilyn Monroe, who died yesterday at thirty-six. Rest in peace, dear one. And in the Long, Deep Sigh Department: Darling Tab Hunter is seeing Naughty Natalie Wood again. But take heart: Tinseltown Tattlers swear that Natalie would and Tab . . . *wouldn't*!"

I pulled into the lot over the black hose that rang a bell. The gas jockey in a gray suit and a tiny cap like a railroad engineer's ran from the glass building, a greasy towel slung over his left shoulder.

He took the Rambler.

I carried my briefcase past the pumps, standing underneath the palms that hung limp in the heat, to the phone booth. I riffled through the white pages that dangled on a chain from the shelf.

The listing was under "Times, Los Angeles," the number Osbrn 9-2527.

I stood at the phone and called.

"*L.A. Times*," the switchboard said.

"Marshall Cantwell, please."

"—second."

A buzzing, followed by a voice: "Cantwell."

"Yes, hi, Mr. Cantwell. This is Ben Fitzgerald down at the County Coroner's? Was wondering if I could ask you a stupid question."

"Sure."

"The time that was printed in your article today, about the Monroe death?"

"What about it?"

"Well, you quoted Mrs. Murray, the housekeeper, as saying that she woke at three A.M. That accurate?"

"Mr. Fitzgerald, I'm a reporter."

"I know. Just wanted to make sure it wasn't a misprint or something. Mrs. Murray told you that she woke at three A.M.?"

"She did."

"Did you talk to Greenson and Engelberg about this?"

"Yes."

"Did they verify the time?"

"Mr. Fitzgerald, I find this line of questioning insulting. You do your job, and I'll do mine."

"Please just answer the question, and then I'll hang up. Did they verify the time?"

"Yes."

He hung up.

I shook my last Kent from the pack in my pocket, but I didn't light it.

It was Day One.

I chewed on the butt, opened the phone book to the M's, but found no listing for a "Eunice Murray." There was an "E A Murray" on Fourth Avenue, and an "E J Murray" on Oxford.

The first was the wrong number. The second didn't answer, so I turned to the G's, my finger going down the names:

"Greenson Ralph R MD": 436 N Roxbury Drive in Beverly Hills.

I dialed CR 1-4050.

A woman answered. "Dr. Greenson's office."

"Dr. Greenson, please."

"The doctor isn't in right now."

"When do you expect him?"

"Not soon. He's on vacation."

"Vacation." I scrawled this on my pad. "When will he return?"

"I'm not sure."

"You're not . . . sure. Are you his secretary?"

"Yes, sir."

"And you're not sure when he's returning?"

She didn't respond.

"What if I had an emergency?"

"*Is* this an emergency?"

"No, but what if?"

"Are you a patient of Dr Greenson's, sir?"

"No, ma'am."

"Would you like to schedule an appointment?"

I hung up, my finger moving down the white pages again to the second number: "Dr. Hyman Engelberg"—9730 Wilshire in Beverly Hills, CRestview 5-4366.

He, too, was on vacation.

"Is the whole world on vacation?" I asked Engelberg's secretary.

"I can't speak for the world, sir. I can only speak for Dr. Engelberg. He's in the Côte d'Azur."

"The Côte d'Azur." I scribbled this on the paper, then called Clemmons.

"Hello?"

"Jack, it's Ben."

"Ben. How's it hanging?"

"To the left. As usual. Look, Jack. Did you see the papers this morning?"

"Of course."

"Then you know what I'm calling about. The timeline changed. Reporter from the paper swears that Greenson, Engelberg, and Murray all told him that Murray woke up around three. They told you *midnight*, though, right?"

I heard him breathing, kids fighting in the background.

"Jack?" I said. "You there?"

"I'm listening."

"You said they told you midnight."

"So?"

"So all three changed their story. First it was midnight. Then it was three. Someone got to them, Jack."

"Fitz, this isn't a great time. We're packing up."

"Packing."

"Taking a few weeks off."

"How nice for you."

"Could really use the break. Get out of this heat."

"Great," I said. "In the Côte d'Azur?"

"Where?"

"You going to the Côte d'Azur?"

"What gave you that idea? Florence, Fitz. We're going to Florence."

"Who's paying for it, Jack?"

"'Scuse me?"

"I said who's paying for your trip?"

"Kinda question is that?"

"Murray told you midnight, Jack. Greenson told you midnight. Engelberg told you midnight. Isn't that right?"

"I don't remember."

"You don't—"

"Does it matter? The poor girl overdosed, for crissakes. All the papers say she overdosed. Who *cares* when they found her? She had a *history* of this. She wasn't *murdered*."

"Who said anything about murder?"

"It's in her history, her genes. Her mother—"

"Who said anything about *murder*, Jack?"

"The truth is that I can't say."

"Jack—"

"The truth is I don't know."

He hung up.

I checked the coin slot for stray dimes, unfolded the doors, and spent thirty-five cents on a fresh pack of Kents from the cigarette machine.

The matchbook, at least, was free.

15.

Verdugo City isn't a city proper so much as a vacant area in the La Crescenta Valley south of the San Gabriels in north Glendale. One of the developers whose ambitious lives stud L.A. history like pushpins on a precinct map decided to build a residential area here. He started with a two-story redbrick post office built at the railway terminus. The development never took off, but the post office still exists. I'd seen it before, on some errand or another, but I couldn't find it that day, as I can't find so much of the L.A. I remember.

The unplanned urban sprawl had grown like an invasive plant around surrounding communities, consuming them with prefab ranch houses and taxes, the whole city built on sand that shifted like its values. Which means that so much of what I remember is gone, and there are days when I wander the bleached streets wishing I had photos of the buildings I'd lived in, trying to remember the location of the ice cream stand where my father once took me, when in fact I'm not sure it was ever there to begin with.

"What does this have to do with anything?" you ask.

"I went out to Verdugo City."

"Why?"

"To find Marilyn's mother. Next of kin, remember? That's how the whole thing started."

Do you have an appointment?" the receptionist asked at the Rockhaven front desk. It was in the alcove of a chintzy waiting room that contained a Bunn coffeemaker and a low table surrounded by a few chairs.

I took my hat off. "No."

"We only admit guests with appointments. Your name again?"

"Fitzgerald."

"I don't see it on this list."

"I'm from the L.A. County Coroner's. I'm looking for next of kin for Norma Jeane Baker. You probably know her as Marilyn Monroe."

"Oh, my." She brightened visibly, adjusting her white shift as if I were about to take her picture. "Well, you'll want to see Gladys, then."

"And Gladys is—?"

"The mother. She's in recreation now, but recess will be over in, I'd say, ten minutes. I'll let them know. Do you mind waiting?"

"Nome."

"Have a seat. Coffee is free."

"Thank you, ma'am."

"Cream's free, too."

The coffee was bad. So was the cream.

I sat on one of the chairs that had been worn over the years by women who waited for people who never arrived and things that never happened. On the table was a plastic ashtray on which the name Rockhaven had been painted in pink brushstrokes by Mexican immigrants in factories just outside town.

"Pardon me?" the receptionist said. "Sir?"

I looked up, toothpick still in my mouth. "Yes?"

"I'm sorry to bother you, but I wondered, did you . . . know Marilyn Monroe? In person, I mean?"

"No."

"Well, I wondered. Because people say I look like her. 'Course I think that's utter nonsense."

"I only ever saw her dead. You don't look like her dead."

"Oh, my."

The manageress emerged from the long hall, like a female (not to say human) ironing board, stiff in her straitjacket suit, and announced that Gladys Morton was "ready" but that I was to "confine myself only to questions of a practical, professional nature."

"I wouldn't think of doing anything else."

"Then you're not like all the others."

"What others?"

"The ones that were here. Asking inappropriate things."

"About what?"

"Come along. She's in the Annex."

The light in the room was cold. The room was cold, too, oddly enough, given the heat. The old woman sat on the edge of the bed in a housecoat, a purse clutched with worn hands below the knees. Her nylons were torn. She wore nice shoes, not slippers. She looked as if she had dressed in "fancy" clothes for lunch at the Folger Café, where she would sip tepid coffee in porcelain cups on saucers bearing the famous faded blue logo. She would order the Fancy Eggs and a slice of the coconut cream pie because, of course, this was a "special occasion."

The bed was small and crisply made. There was nothing else in the room but a dresser and a mirror turned to the wall. And a bedside table: a fringed lamp, a water glass, a copy of Mary Baker Eddy's *Science and Health with Key to the Scriptures.*

"She thinks," said the manageress who'd brought me to this room, "she's going shopping, don't you, Gladys?"

Gladys did not look up. She had the long empty stare of schizophrenia. Mental illness ran like a virus in the family. We know that now. Gladys's sick mother killed herself. Gladys herself believed that men were following her, lurking outside every window, behind every door.

She had to double-check her closet before bed every night.

"When she isn't frightened," the woman whispered to me, "she simply isn't here."

I wondered what sort of burden that would be: panic the high price of feeling alive. In the absence of fright, there is only the void she was clearly in then, staring without blinking at a spot on the floor.

"Gladys?" the woman said. "Aren't you? Going shopping."

Gladys looked up. "I have my list."

"This nice young man may be willing to help you."

The old woman's face darted up to mine. The movement seemed mechanical, more vegetable than human. "I don't *want* him to help me."

"He just wants to ask you some questions, dear. Surely you can answer some questions for him."

Gladys's head turned back to the floor.

There was nothing there.

"He believes in God," the manageress said, finally.

Gladys looked up. "What kind of God?"

"The *only* God," I said.

"Amen," she said, explaining that signs in the sky proved that God existed and showed his pure love. Spiders on the wall like the ones you could see were merely God in disguise. God had not absented himself from the world that he loved so well and so truly well. The proof was everywhere that God was everywhere. Even in the smallest things. *Especially* in the smallest things.

"Amen," I said.

"Like *that*." She pointed to a stain on the floor.

"I need to tell you something, ma'am," I said.

"Tell me what you know." She looked into my eyes for the first time. Her gaze was empty. Her finger was still pointing.

"Your daughter," I said, "has died. Is dead. She's dead."

"My daughter?"

"Norma Jeane."

"I don't remember. I don't recall."

"Marilyn Monroe. Her name was Marilyn Monroe."

"I have never heard," she said, "of Marilyn Monroe."

16.

REPORT OF CHEMICAL ANALYSIS

LOS ANGELES COUNTY CORONER
Toxicology Laboratory
Hall of Justice
Los Angeles, California

File No. 81128 I

Name of Deceased: Marilyn Monroe

Date Submitted: August 6, 1962 Time: 8 A.M.

Autopsy Surgeon: T. Noguchi, M.D.

Material Submitted:

Blood x	Liver x	Stomach x
Brain	Lung	Lavage
Femur	Spleen	Urine x
Kidney x	Sternum	Gall bladder
Drugs x	Chemicals	Intestines x

Test Desired: Ethanol, Barbiturates

Laboratory Findings:

Blood: Ethanol — Absent

Blood: Barbiturates — 4.5 mg. per cent
Phenobarbital is absent

Drugs:
(1) 27 capsules, #19295, 6-7-62, Librium, 5 mgm. #50
(2) 17 capsules, 20201, 7-10-62, Librium, 10 mgm. #100
(3) 26 tablets, #20569, 7-25-62, Sulfathallidine, #36
(4) Empty container, #20858, 8-3-62, Nembutal, 1½gr.#25
(5) 10 green capsules, #20570, 7-31-62, Chloral Hydrate 0.5 gm. #50 (Refill: 7-25-62 - original)
(6) Empty container, #456099, 11-4-61, Noludar, #50
(7) 32 pink capsules in a container without label Phenergan, #20857, 8-3-62, 25 mg. #25
(

Examined By R.J. Abernethy Head Toxicologist. Date August 6, 1962

That was the first iteration of the tox report. A revision, with minor corrections, followed later that day:

REPORT OF CHEMICAL ANALYSIS
LOS ANGELES COUNTY CORONER
Toxicology Laboratory
Hall of Justice
Los Angeles, California

File No. 81128 I

Name of Deceased Marilyn Monroe 1st Supplement

Date Submitted August 6, 1962 Time 8 A.M.

Autopsy Surgeon T. Noguchi, M.D.

Material Submitted:

Blood x	Liver x	Stomach x
Brain	Lung	Lavage
Femur	Spleen	Urine x
Kidney x	Sternum	Gall bladder
Drugs x	Chemicals	Intestines x

Test Desired. Chloral Hydrate, Pentobarbital

Laboratory Findings:

Blood: Chloral Hydrate 8 mg. per cent

Liver: Pentobarbital 13.0 mg. per cent

Drugs: Correction - delete #7 on original report of August 6 and add:

(7) 32 peach-colored tablets marked MSD in prescriptic type vial without label.

(8) 24 white tablets #20857, 8-3-62, Phenergan, 25 mg. #25

(SEE ORIGINAL REPORT)

Examined By R. J. Abernethy, Head Toxicologist. Date August 13, 1962

Now, you want to know what this report means, Doc. Well, it was clear that Miss Monroe's death had been caused by a massive overdose—4.5 milligrams barbs and 8 milligrams chloral. Her liver contained 13 mg pentobarbital, or Nembutal.

And that was troubling.

"Why?" you ask.

I looked for the specimen analyses that Noguchi had requested. Ralph Abernethy, the chief toxicologist, had delivered analyses on the blood and liver, but Noguchi had requested analyses on the kidney, stomach, urine, and intestines as well. It was in the autopsy report. He'd requested them because the analysis of all these organs would show exactly how barbiturates had entered the system.

But it wasn't there.

"Without specimen analysis, Doctor, there's no way of telling how the pills were ingested."

"Why does that matter? She killed herself, Ben."

"*Did* she?"

"Everyone says she killed herself."

"I'm not everyone."

I picked up the phone and called—

"Noguchi," said the voice on the other end.

"Morning, Doctor. It's Ben. I don't see all the specimen analyses on the tox report."

"I know. I asked Dr. Abernethy for them again."

"Why didn't he do them in the first place?"

"He said it was obviously an overdose."

"It wasn't obviously anything."

"So you say."

"Where is Dr. Abernethy now?"

"*You* know," he said. "The press conference."

. . .

"From information supplied to us, we feel we can make a presumptive opinion that Miss Monroe did not die of natural causes," Curphey said as I stepped into the room on the fifth floor. I propped myself against the wall, searching for Abernethy among the rows of reporters on folding chairs, public officials, some taking notes, others snapping pictures.

I was chewing a toothpick.

Curphey sat behind a mass of microphones in his coroner whites. The table was covered with a cloth; a pitcher of water sat in the middle. He was flanked by three men. Behind them stood a cop.

"The cause of death was a massive overdose of barbiturates," he continued. "Chief toxicologist R. J. Abernethy found four-point-five milligrams of barbiturate poisoning per one hundred cc's of blood, about twice what we'd consider a lethal dose. The exact type of drug ingested by Miss Monroe has not been determined.

"Her death will be probed by my office and by the Los Angeles Suicide Prevention Team, the independent investigating unit of the Los Angeles Suicide Prevention Center at UCLA. I'd like to think of this as the 'suicide squad.' Through this organ, we will hold exhaustive interviews regarding the probable suicide of Marilyn Monroe. And now." He cleared his throat. "I'd like to introduce you to the team."

Dr. Robert Litman was a psychiatrist and UCLA professor who had studied under Dr. Greenson.

Dr. Norman Farberow was a psychologist and the nominal head of the Suicide Squad.

Dr. Norman Tabachnick was yet another associate of Greenson's.

"We will take a psychiatric approach to the case," Curphey said. "This involves delving delicately but thoroughly into Miss Monroe's personal history. We're interviewing everybody. We'll seek out all persons with whom Miss Monroe had recently been associated." There would be, he said, "no limitations" to the scope of their inquiry; the team "would go as far back in her life as necessary."

"Dr. Curphey!" a voice from the crowd.

I looked across the chairs and saw Jo Carnahan. She sat in the middle of the row. She wore a waistless chemise with a chain belt and a gold evening bag. She held a reporter's notebook and a pen.

I *still* didn't know who she reminded me of.

"I'm sorry." Curphey squinted against the light. "I haven't opened up the floor to questions. Now, we will be very thorough in our treatment of this. It is obviously—"

"Dr. Curphey," Jo said again. "How could she have swallowed the pills when there was no water glass?"

"I beg your pardon?"

"There was no water glass in Miss Monroe's room. If the verdict is that she took a handful of sleeping pills, why was there no water glass in the room?"

"Ma'am—"

"The name is Jo Carnahan."

"Miss Carnahan, I am not a detective. I am the coroner. I do not speak as an expert when I say that we can have no idea at this juncture *how* Miss Monroe ingested the pills. She could in fact have chewed them."

"She *chewed* fifty pills?"

"We don't know the exact count, Miss Carnahan. In any event, there was a water glass. I myself saw it. There are photos of it. It was empty."

"But Mr. Curphey—"

"I haven't opened the floor to questions, Miss Carnahan."

The cop behind Curphey stepped into the crowd, moved down

the aisle, and motioned for Jo to leave. There were hushed words. Jo refused to move; the cop grabbed Jo's arm, muttering things I couldn't hear as he tugged at her. She wasn't leaving, though: "Mr. Curphey—"

"*Dr.* Curphey," he corrected.

"You haven't answered my question."

All the cameras turned to Jo, flashing as she was pulled from the aisle down the hall to the door.

I followed her.

None of this showed up in the papers the next day, by the way. You should know that. They all reported on the conference, dutifully repeating the self-serving things Curphey had said, and though at least a hundred pictures had been taken of Jo being yanked from the building, not a single one was published. They didn't mention Jo, the empty glass—or the fact that her nose was bleeding.

She stormed through the parking lot along Spring, clutching a manila envelope under her right arm.

"Ma'am," I said, following her. I was grinning. I don't know why. Something about her—

"Go away."

"Name's Fitzgerald. Deputy coroner."

"Sure, I remember. The bright boy who kicked me from the death house yesterday."

"You weren't supposed to be there."

"And you weren't supposed to steal the tissue samples."

"I *didn't* steal the tissue samples."

"That's what you testified."

"I was doing my job."

"So was I."

"Need a tissue?"

"You mean a sample?"

"I mean a Kleenex."

"I need you to get lost."

She stopped at her DeSoto, a candy-apple '61. She took the keys from her gold purse.

"I know why there was no water glass," I said.

She froze. Very slowly, she straightened. She turned. "What?"

"I said: I know why there was no water glass."

"Really. Tell me."

"If I show you mine," I said, "will you show me yours?"

"Depends."

"On what?"

"How big it is."

It was big. You know how big it was, Doctor.

"Well, I'm famished," she said. "You want lunch?"

"I could eat a horse."

"Right. So how do you feel about chili?"

17.

Hello, Tommy," she said as the waiter arrived at our booth. He wore a black tux and tie, but his front teeth protruded and his Ken-doll hair was combed over a bald spot. He didn't look like he worked at a joint where they treated food like paper dolls, dressing rib bones up in ribbons, torturing carrots and radishes into tiny swans, Eiffel Towers, and the constellation of Orion.

"Afternoon, Miss Carnahan," he said. He deposited a basket of warm cheese toast on the white tablecloth. "And how are we today?"

"It's too soon to tell. Two Flames, please," Jo said, waving across the tables to the bartender, who was laboring over some bright concoction under rows of winking wineglasses.

"Cigarette?" She took a pack of Kools from her gold bag, removed one with the red nails that exactly matched her lips, and held it out to me.

"No thanks. Trying to quit."

"Suit yourself." She slipped it into her mouth. She had a way of making ordinary gestures seem obscene. It had something to do with her amused deliberation and something else to do with her eyes.

I took her lighter and lit the cigarette, and when she lifted her white neck to blow smoke toward the ceiling, I knew who she reminded me of:

"Vivien Leigh," I said.

"Excuse me?"

"Never mind."

Chasen's was the large green awning on Beverly Boulevard. You always saw the limos parked outside, swells parading past flanks of reporters elbowing one another for the best shots, the diamonds and white furs of Elizabeth Taylor and Natalie Wood, the white tuxedo shirts of Jimmy Stewart and Rock Hudson. They were all blurs against the doors that opened for them, as they'd opened for us, that day, Dave Chasen himself saying, "Afternoon, Miss Carnahan," and whisking us past the picture of W. C. Fields to the booth where we now sat.

"Miss Carnahan?" I said.

"Jo."

"With all due respect, Jo: Why do you care what happened to Marilyn Monroe? I mean, I know your show and column. It's fluff. Women's magazine stuff. Good guys and bad guys. Stars we love on the way up and then shoot down."

"So?"

"Why are you so interested in the water glass?"

Jo blew smoke from her mouth toward the ceiling.

"I went to convent school in New York. I was a good Irish Catholic girl. A daddy's girl. Maybe all Catholic girls are. I wanted to cover news, but that's hard for a girl, so I wrote about a convention of beauty parlor owners for the *Evening Journal*, the opening of a model home in Flatbush. I interviewed the highest tenants in the Empire State Building and Leontyne Price. It wasn't what I wanted."

"What did you want?"

"Crime. Politics. Business. Big stories. The Boy stories. But water seeks its own level, and a woman isn't water, but she's treated like it."

"So?"

"The Annie Laurie job opened. I wanted to leave New York. I wasn't getting anywhere. It was more money. And I like to think I've added some dimension to the character. I came up with the phrase 'dear ones.' And 'the Long, Deep Sigh Department.' That was my idea. It's one of the most popular segments."

"But you still—"

"You know how they say 'once a Catholic, always a Catholic'?"

"Sure."

"Once a journalist, always a journalist. I happen to be both."

She took from her manila envelope an 8 × 10 glossy she'd developed at the *Mirror*:

Monroe's bedside table, covered with vials. Underneath was a Mexican pottery jug, cap askew, piles of books and papers and a jar of face cream, but—

"No water glass," I said.

"Bingo."

It was not what I had seen at the house, Doc: On the table by the bed I'd seen the same vial of pills, the same books and papers, the same jar of night cream—and an empty glass.

"Somehow between the time I took this picture and the time that you arrived, Ben, a glass showed up on the table. Someone put it there. I didn't think there was anything suspicious about the death until that happened. I'm looking around, and the first thing I think is: If this is an overdose, where's the water?"

"They turned it off the night before. The renovations."

"So how'd she swallow the pills?"

"I don't think she *swallowed* anything."

"Come again?"

"She had four-point-five percent milligrams of barbiturates and eight percent chloral hydrate in her bloodstream."

"I heard."

"That means she needed to swallow around thirty to forty Nembutals. And *that* doesn't even account for the thirteen percent pentobarbital Dr. Abernethy also found in the liver. When you consider the liver—"

"I was considering the chili."

"When you consider the liver, it means that an additional twenty or so capsules and tablets had to have been ingested. That means, Miss Carnahan—"

"Jo."

"That means, Jo, that case number 81128 had to have consumed at least fifty, if not eighty, pills to die."

"But she *did* die."

"The point is we're assuming she consumed them *by mouth*."

"So?"

"So even if she'd had a water glass, even if she'd drunk a gallon of water, she couldn't have swallowed those pills."

"I could swallow that basket of toast."

"It's not the same thing. The pills are poison. The body rejects them. You vomit them up."

She glanced back at the menu. "Maybe I won't have the chili after all."

"We found nothing in her digestive tract," I said. "Not even a yellow stain."

"Why would you find that?"

"Nembutals are known as 'yellow jackets,' 'cause of their deep color. If Miss Monroe had somehow swallowed, say, thirty-six of them, her digestive tract would have been stained yellow—but there was no color," I said. "And no refractile crystals."

"Refractive what?"

"*Refractile.* If you ingest more than twelve capsules of barbiturates, refractile crystals show up in the digestive tract or in the stomach."

"Please use English, please."

"That's refractile crystals. Meaning . . . I don't know . . . they refract."

"And that means?"

"Subject to refraction."

"Oh. Jesus."

"It means they have the power to change the direction of the ray of light."

"You mean they reflect."

"You could say that."

"Well, why didn't you?"

"Two Flames of Love," Tommy said, carefully depositing two martini glasses filled with Pepe's house special: vodka, "La Ina" Fino Sherry, and burned orange peel.

Jo's eyes sparkled as she extended her glass to mine.

The glasses touched. We drank.

"So you're telling me that you don't think she killed herself?"

It's not my business to speculate (I told her, as I'm telling you, Doc), but in the entire history of forensics, no one has ever died with such high blood concentrations of phenobarb and chloral hydrate as a result of *oral* ingestion.

"Then why did she leave a suicide note?" she asked.

"She didn't."

"Oh, really?" She took a piece of paper from that same manila envelope.

It was a page torn from the diary.

"You took this from the death scene?" I asked.

She nodded.

"You know that's illegal."

"You gonna arrest me?"

"Maybe."

The paper was covered with illegible writing and crossed-off numbers. The only words I could read were "The enemy within."

"What the hell does that mean?" I asked.

"I wish I knew," Jo said. "It was lying on her pillow, as if she'd tried to call someone."

"She was calling the Justice Department."

"How do you know?"

"She left the number in her diary. I read it."

"How?"

"I took it."

"Now who's going to get arrested?" she said. "You *took* the diary?"

I nodded. "I have it right here."

18.

May 16, 1962. Forgive me but it was all I ever wanted. I tried so many times but never with results and always with pain, well, once I almost died but this will be different and will change everything, the one who will have the things I never had and see the things I never saw and be loved and safe and sane and mine.

[redacted], forgive me: [redacted]

But it started and I was excited and then it ended again like before. The General just stopped calling. It was just like his brother all over again. He gave me a number and told me to use the name of Mrs. Green but first the woman on the other end said she didn't know a Mrs. Green and then it just stopped working.

Mrs. Green is what he told me to tell them like a secret that we shared, like with so many others, in bed. But now he's not here. He never is. Like the Commander. Marilyn Monroe is a soldier but what good is a soldier without a commander?

I started calling the *other* number the public one saying I was Mrs. Green. I looked it up in the book:

RE7-8200

RE7-8200

RE7-8200

It was like before. "I need to speak to him!" I said and all that. "He owes me! You understand?"

I believe he loved me or was falling in love with me I don't believe it was just what they call "pillow talk" when he said that he would leave his wife and kids. He meant it or his *dick* did, Diary!!!!

But someone got to him. His brother or wife? The woman who is calling me at night? Diary, I DON'T sleep but now there is the ringing of the pink phone at 1 and 3 a.m. someone on the other end saying, "Stay away from [redacted]."

You see how they removed that and how they crossed it out? I didn't do that. I wrote the name but when I woke in the morning it was gone.

Maybe it is the man at the window.

He should face me and tell me why. Or tell me on the phone. I don't care. I just want to know *why*.

An hour ago I called the number asked for him again and they said he wasn't there again and asked to take a message. "Boy, I'll give you a message tell him [redacted] and [redacted] clicks on my phone and [redacted] is bugging my house on account of they want information. Did you get that? Can you spell that, Angie?"

"I can spell that."

"Tell him if he doesn't call me back I will call a press conference. Have you got that?"

"I got that."

"I could blow this whole thing sky-high."

Yes there are the clicks the sound of clicking on the phone and voices like people whispering in the background like they're listening and something rustling in my closet the clack-clack of empty hangers there. The water is wrong but the man who came to fix it didn't. Eunice said that he was there and something tells me he is STILL!!!

I'm TIRED of being used TIRED of being treated like an animal. WORSE than an animal!!!!

God it's too hot to sleep and I know something's going to happen and then there's the bottle of pills.

Three more would help or thirty.

And now the phone is ringing

The phone," Jo said.

I looked up from the diary. "What about it?"

"She lived and died on the phone. She was clutching it in her hand."

"So?"

"Did anyone go to GTE?"

"What's that?"

"General Telephone. Did anyone check the phone records?"

"Aren't *you* the journalist?"

"Don't answer a question with a question," she said as she stood from the table.

19.

A guy at GTE named George agreed to meet us in the Service Room to tell us what he didn't want to tell us (he said) on the phone. But the fact is that he *didn't* meet us in the Service Room. When we showed up, the woman behind the long counter said that George was still at lunch. It was strange for him, she said, as he was a man of routine.

"Where does he usually lunch?" Jo asked.

"The Tip Top on Melrose. Always at the same time. And he always has the same thing: the corned beef sandwich on rye. I should know. I've worked here twenty years."

"Thanks." Jo turned to go.

"You want to talk to him?"

"Yes."

"Try the Benson Bar on Fifth."

"You said he takes his lunch at Tip Top."

"You asked where he *usually* takes his lunch, but today he's at the Benson." She checked her watch. "He's usually back by one-thirty."

"Time is it now?"

"Almost three."

Just then I remembered something: "Jesus."

"What?"

"I need to pick up Max."

"Max?"

"My son. He's at school."

"You're married?"

"Almost."

"What does that mean, *almost*?"

"Call me," I said. "I'm at the Savoy."

I parked across the street in the rain. The buses were gone. The classes were over, the flag off the pole. Two stragglers left with their parents in yellow raincoats, holding umbrellas over their heads. I remembered a drawing Max had once done showing clouds and the moon and the rain. "Ligting comes with rain," he'd written. "Ligting is dangerous."

Max didn't have a raincoat. Or an umbrella. He didn't have boots, either.

I pushed through the double doors into the lobby, blinking against the water that dripped from my hair. The school smelled like all schools smell in the rain, wet cotton mixed with chlorine from an unseen pool. The trophy cases were filled with dusty mementos of teachers who had died and of spelling bees won. The floor was covered with boot prints.

The sign on the first door to the left, the one before the hall of lockers, read PRINCIPAL in gold letters.

"I'm looking for my son," I said to the woman behind the desk. Cat's-eye glasses hung on a chain around her neck. A series of cubicles flanked a narrow hall that led to the only room with a view. On the door, a sign showed two kids with googly eyes: "THE PRINCIPAL IS YOUR *PAL*!" it read.

"And his name would be?"

"Max Fitzgerald."

"And he's in? Whose class?"

"Third grade. He's a third-grader."

"His teacher's name?"

"Starts with a *W*."

"That won't help much. We have several *W*'s."

"Wallace? Wilson?"

"We have a Weston. Williams. And a Wettergren." She frowned, put those glasses on the bridge of her nose, and looked up at me over the frames.

"I think it's Wettergren. I'm pretty sure it's—"

"Mrs. Wettergren's class has all gone, I'm afraid. They've *all* gone home."

"I was supposed to pick him up."

"Your son: Max Fitzgerald. Is he the handsome little boy—"

"Of course."

"The one who didn't have a raincoat?"

"I didn't know it would be raining."

"The weather report is quite simple, sir. He didn't have an umbrella, either. Or boots."

"I didn't know he needed—"

"He waited in the rain for thirty minutes, Mr. . . . Fitzgerald."

"Ben."

"Mrs. Wettergren stayed with the umbrella. Your wife—"

"I didn't know."

"She came to pick him up."

"I'm sorry. May I use your phone?"

"There's a pay phone in the lobby."

I dropped the dime. Pressed the phone to my ear. And dialed into silence.

I hit the coin return. I didn't care about the rain now. I walked down the sidewalk to the car across the street.

A parking ticket sat under the wind wings.

I waited in the car outside the house. No one was home. I waited with the diary and the ticket and the Kents in the glove compartment and the radio on that station. I kept staring through the path the wipers cut in the rain. I stared, too, through the window up the driveway to the garage, wondering when Rose would return.

I'd fucked up and knew it. I just wanted to apologize.

The house was not, unlike most in El Segundo, Spanish Colonial. It was something more "modern," a polite term for prefab: a barn-red ranch with aluminum siding, a porch in the back with garden hoses underneath and fences on both sides of the lawn.

I waited.

5:15 P.M.: "Real friends were almost unanimous in saying they believed that her death was accidental," the radio voice said through static. "Two motion pictures executives were bidding for her services at the time of her death. Miss Monroe had received an offer of fifty-five thousand dollars a week to star in a nightclub appearance in Las Vegas."

I kept switching stations, trying to get away from the story that had already killed everything, but no one could talk about anything else. Even in Titusville, they were talking:

"I am sure it was an accident," Dean Martin said at 8:26 P.M. "She was at my home just a few days ago. She was happy, in excellent spirits, and we were making plans to resume the picture early next year. She was a warm, wonderful person. The only one she ever hurt was herself."

1:01 A.M.: I drove back to the Savoy and lit a cigarette.

Tomorrow would be Day One.

20.

"*Buenas noches*, Señor Ben," Inez said from behind the bar. She was serving beer to Elisha Cook, Jr., or someone who looked like him. It was hard to tell in the bad light, but the presence of this man was a measure of how far the place had fallen.

The Savoy had once been a playground for Hollywood's celluloid set, back when mid-Wilshire had been the Center of the Film World, the Oscars at the Ambassador, Joan Crawford dancing under fake palms at the Cocoanut Grove. The bar off the lobby had featured a dance floor on springs where showgirls kicked, chosen for no reason other than the fact that their breasts looked great in pasties. But it wasn't long before their eyes were as dead as the dreams that had led to nothing but the snapped spine of a lemon in the bottom of a gin glass.

After a few suspicious fires, the Savoy went from a palace to a sad place that traded in human remnants, pornographic pictures, and flagons of ether and laudanum. The butts of cheap cigarettes sizzled in the gin as the girls picked up their plastic clutches, slid off their respective stools, and followed the latest johns straight up the stairs.

You always had to take the stairs.

The elevator never worked.

It still didn't.

"A lady call for you," Inez said.

"A lady?"

"With a man's name. She call two time. Say it is about phone records. She say to tell you, mmm, *no sé como se dice* . . ."

She handed me the message on a piece of notebook paper:

"Joe Carnahan," it read. "'Not even Jay Edgar Hoover.' "

"What does that mean, Inez?"

"*No sé*, Señor Ben."

"She didn't say?"

"No. There was a man come, too."

"What man?"

"To fix your doorbell."

"Doorbell isn't broken."

"Yes it is, okay. He say you call. You pay for it, okay."

"I didn't pay for anything," I said. "Where was he from?"

"The doorbell company."

"There's no such thing. How long was he here?"

She shrugged. "Twenty minutes."

"And he was in my room?"

"Yes."

"He was alone?"

"Don't be mad, Señor Ben."

"I'm not mad, Inez, it's just . . . Don't let anyone inside the apartment unless I give you permission, okay?"

"He say he have your permission. He have the work order, okay."

She handed me the work order:

B. F. FOX ELECTRIC
4100 S La Cienega Blvd
Baldwin Hills

For work completed Aug 6:
installation of new doorbell.
Due upon receipt: $13.45

"Señor Ben?"

"Yes."

"*¿Eres un hombre bueno, sí?* Your wife should know that."

"*No entiendo.*"

"You are a good man," she said. "Whatever else you do. You have a good heart and soul, señor."

"*Gracias*, Inez. I appreciate it."

"But you have terrible taste in women."

I hardly slept that night. I kept thinking of Jo and Max and Rose and the phone records. Insomnia seeped through the vents that made the rushing sounds you hear when the traffic stops except for the sirens, except for all the rain. It rained a lot that year. Insomnia was layered in the sand that came from over the Mohave through the window. The sand was trapped, along with the smell of smoke, in the carpet, no matter how many times I tried to vacuum it up. No matter that I always kept the windows closed.

But it was more than that.

"Now you're getting carried away," you say. "And too florid. It's a common thing in addicts."

"I'm not an addict."

"Just tell me what happened."

When I went upstairs, the door to 7-A was open, Doctor, and all the lights were on, but I didn't see anything missing or misplaced. There was nothing *to* miss or misplace. I could have made the case that the level of milk in the kitchenette was lower than usual, but that may have been my imagination, as you suppose so much is.

"I don't *suppose*," you say.

The bare light over the table off the kitchenette was on, and it swung slightly, as if someone had just touched it, but everything else seemed normal. The toilet was still running. The bed was unmade.

The doorbell rang.

I pressed the intercom: "Yes?"

"Señor Ben, it's Inez. You see?"

"See what?"

"The doorbell works. They fix it."

"It wasn't broken," I said.

It was 2:15.

TUESDAY, AUGUST 7

21.

The heat wave continued in Southland. It was eighty-nine in L.A., ninety-plus in San Gabriel and San Fernando. It was ninety-two at the Civic Center, humidity at forty-one. That's what they said on the radio. The papers were still filled with Marilyn news: preparations for the funeral, Curphey's press conference, interviews with the hairdressers and stylists who'd Known Her Well.

A story in the *Times* gave the first complete chronology of her last day: Everyone claimed that she had seemed "happy." Her press agent, Pat Newcomb, had spent the night before in the Telephone Room. And Marilyn had spent a sleepless night in her own bedroom, on the phone. That morning, the actress asked for oxygen, the Hollywood cure for a hangover. There was no oxygen, so she drank grapefruit juice instead. She shared it with Newcomb; at some point, they argued. Newcomb said that the argument was about the fact that she herself had slept all night but Marilyn had not.

"You gonna pay for that paper, or aren't you?" the man behind the newsstand asked. He wore a visor over a balding head. Nudie magazines hung on a sagging wash line behind him.

"Sorry." I reached into my pockets and found nothing. "Be right back." I handed him the paper.

"You already read half of what it's worth."

"Not true," I said. "I didn't read the funnies."

The jukebox was running, but no one was in the bar. Elisha Cook, Jr., and Inez were long gone. The ripped leather booths were empty, the candles on the dark scored tables unlit. A silver bell for service sat on the shelf of the alcove. I rang it but no one came. I took my hat off and slid it along the bar wood. The clock on the wall read 8:12—late enough to call home.

I stepped behind the bar and grabbed the phone. I thought about smoking a cigarette, but decided against it.

It was Day One.

Rose: "Hello?"

"It's Ben."

She didn't say a thing, so I said it again: "It's Ben."

"I heard you the first time. Jesus, Ben. What happened?"

"I showed up at the house last night, and you weren't there."

"Oh? And where were you when you were supposed to pick up Max?"

"I don't know what to say. I mean I'm sorry."

"You should be sorry to Max. *He's* the one you abandoned."

"I didn't abandon anyone."

"Standing alone on the sidewalk in the rain waiting for his daddy after all the other kids had gone? He drew a crayon picture for you, Ben. He wanted you to see it."

"I just want to say I'm sorry to—"

"A crayon picture," she said. "For *you*."

"Rose, I'm onto something. If you knew the truth, you'd understand."

She didn't respond.

"Rose?"

She had hung up.

I lit a cigarette.

Tomorrow would be—

You know.

I called Jo.

"Ben!" she said. "I've been trying to reach you."

"I know. You left a message."

"So I went to see our dear friend George from GTE in the bar. He told me that all hell has broken loose. Marilyn's phone records have disappeared."

"I'm sure the police—"

"It wasn't the police. This is where it gets interesting. He told me that toll calls are recorded by hand at the traffic center and filed in boxes that are picked up every night and taken to headquarters. Once they're there, you can't access them. Same thing happens with the calls you dial. They refer to them as—let me read my writing here—Measured Message Unit calls. Well, those are recorded on a yellow tape roll, whatever that means, and *that* ends up in lockdown, too."

"So?"

"So no ordinary cop would be able to get ahold of those records after they were filed. He said, 'Not even J. Edgar Hoover.' "

"What does that mean?"

"Not even J. Edgar Hoover, he said, could get access to those records after they had been filed. But someone did. Someone at the very highest level wanted access to those phone records."

"To be the first to see them?"

"To make sure that no one else did."

. . .

Baldwin Hills is named after the range that overlooks the L.A. basin and the lower plain to the north. It's bordered on the southeast by Leimert Park, on the south by Windsor Hills, on the north by the Mid City, on the west by Culver City.

There are active oil wells in the mid hills along La Cienega, but most of the derricks in the area are rusting, which is what I discovered when I parked on the drive below the hill and walked to the fence at the top. I put my fingers through the links and stared. There was a lot of bleached dirt and dust but no office. And no B. F. Fox Electric.

I looked at the, *como se dice*, work order in my hand and checked the address: 4100 S La Cienega Blvd.

It was the right address, but nothing was here.

The last few entries in the diary of Marilyn Monroe—I now know—were often elliptical, drug-addled, hard to parse or even read. It was sometimes difficult to understand what she was trying to communicate, even harder to understand the connection between the final entries and whatever she'd meant when she'd written "the enemy within."

But the guiding spirit of the thing was paranoia, her belief that she was being watched and bugged and followed. She was consumed by night terrors regarding the phone calls and the clicking on the line and the man outside her window; she often locked her door, as she had the night she died, because she believed the man had gotten inside the house.

Now a strange man was visiting my house to fix a doorbell that wasn't broken. I'd seen no evidence of a break-in and no evidence of the man the night before—until I returned to the Savoy that morning around 10:30.

I ran water in the bathroom sink and rolled my sleeves up and squirted what was left of the Barbasol on my stubble and reached for the Wade & Butcher straight razor that was always to the right of the sink.

But it wasn't to the right of the sink. I stared into the mirror and opened the medicine cabinet.

I didn't find my razor.

What I found was a bottle of Nembutals.

22.

Throughout LACCO, there were old-fashioned post-office mailboxes painted green. In them, we put the evidence of the dead in sealed envelopes, writing descriptions on clipboards tied to the tops with strings: nail clippings, hair samples, bullets.

Someone from the Evidence Division would empty all the boxes at day's end, collect the envelopes, and deliver them to Carl, the evidence tech. He was the only one with the key to the Sheriff's Evidence Room, which, among other things, contained all evidence pertaining to the death of Miss Monroe.

He was sitting behind his desk when I found him, that day, feet up on a row of files, watching *Yours for a Song*. He was singing along with Bert Parks while eating a sandwich. I stepped inside. He didn't hear me: "Toot, Toot, Tootsie," he sang.

"Excuse me."

He turned, chewing, and took his feet off the filing cabinets.

"Sorry. I'm Ben Fitzgerald. Deputy coroner."

"Deputy?" He bit into his sandwich again. "How can I help you?"

"I need to get into the Evidence Room."

"Why?"

"I have a problem."

"Kind of problem?"

I showed him the vial of Nembutals.

"Lots of people have that problem. My wife can't sleep, either."

"The problem is these aren't *my* Nembutals."

"Whose are they?"

"Marilyn Monroe's."

He lowered his sandwich. He stopped chewing. "Not possible."

"Look at the label: 'Dr. Hyman Engelberg. San Vicente Pharmacy.' "

"Jesus," he said.

It was a windowless warehouse in the subbasement. The ceilings were so high and dark you couldn't see them. The few functioning lights sparked in the water that dripped even when it wasn't raining. Aisles were stacked with moldering evidence from ten thousand forgotten cases on high metal shelving: everything from a bullet or a matchbook with an address in a white folder labeled "Vergie, 6/23/27" to a chandelier or a chair, a mirror or some flooring stained, long ago, with blood.

And then there were the stoned rats with pink eyes and ropey tails, whiskery noses that twitched when they rose on hind legs, forepaws hooked like claws. They loved the bags of marijuana confiscated from the Mexicans on, say, Figueroa. They ate through almost anything to get the stuff; you'd see them staggering, stoned, along the floor.

"Here you go," Carl said, handing me the key at the front door. His voice echoed. "Just lock up and return it when you're done. This place gives me the creeps."

"Sure."

"Don't let them bite," he said, and shut the door. I heard him laughing down the hall as I looked at the log he had given me:

CASE NO.: 81128

DECEDENT NAME: Marilyn Monroe

CONTENTS:

1. **A vial of 25 Nembutal capsules from San Vicente Pharmacy**
2. **A vial of ten chloral hydrate tablets filled on July 25**
3. **A small key with a red plastic cover labeled "15"**
4. **The water glass**

LOCATION: Box 24, Row 13-B

I located the southernmost row and counted over to row 13 (where the B came in, I had no idea). But I found nothing—until, twenty minutes later, I came across *The Book of the Unknown Dead* lodged within a stack of mildewed files.

I'd heard tales of this volume, a large black scrapbook started by an assistant, his name lost to history, in 1921. It was a book into which that first man, and many who came after, put evidence from and pictures of people the coroner's office could never identify. These people were all poor, nameless, and alone.

There were pictures of a wino they'd found off Alameda, a black man in a zoot suit in the bathroom of Club Alabam, a hairless man found lying in the reservoir, hobos sliced in half on railroad tracks, floaters washed up in Marina del Rey . . .

"What does this have to do with Monroe?" you ask.

"I thought you would be interested."

"Why?"

"Because of my father."

"I don't want to know about your father. I want to know about the evidence. Did you find it?"

The answer is yes, though it took me a while: The envelope had been misfiled. It was not in Box 24, Row 13-B. It was in Box *25*, Row 13-*C*. And, of course, the vial of Nembutal was missing.

There was just one item inside. It was stuck in the back. I couldn't dislodge it. I turned it over, shook again, and it fell to the floor.

It wasn't really evidence.

It had nothing to do with Miss Monroe.

It was my Wade & Butcher razor.

23.

You want to know how my razor ended up in the evidence folder for Coroner's Case No. 81128? I wish I could tell you.

"So what did you do next?" you ask.

"Went back to my office."

"Why didn't you call the evidence tech?"

"And tell him that my razor had ended up in the Evidence Room? Would *you* believe that?"

"No."

"You'd think I'd put it there myself. What other explanation is there?"

"You're not answering my question, Ben."

More than once my father would leave empty beer cans that weren't really empty around the hotel rooms we shared in Bunker Hill, San Bernardino, and La Habra. Or he and some woman he'd picked up in a Vernon bar would kill half a bottle of rotgut from a package store and he would teach her dance steps to the music that came from whatever faded radio sat by the side of the bed. Very early on I tried tasting the stuff that seemed to work like magic on my father and all these random women. And, though it made me gag at first, it didn't take long to realize that the sickness you felt disappeared fast enough if you swallowed it. It became something more than warm and more than soothing. It changed the way you thought about yourself.

It changed the world.

Mornings, my father always grabbed the Benzedrine that he would buy in tubes and, swallowing the soaked paper inside, he would say, "I will never do this again." He always seemed to mean it, but it happened anyway. It happened because the lights were blooming in the restaurants and taverns. They made the trash cans and alleys between bars look good, and he knew that just one drink would kill the haze, making everything better and clear. Would allow him, finally, to sort out what was wrong and give him the strength to continue.

Not merely to continue: to thrive.

I don't need to tell my story here. You're not interested. Neither am I. All you need to know is that he was working as a bean huller in San Bernardino when he disappeared. He got a bean hull in the eye. You almost couldn't tell the eye was no good, when the doctor was through with it, but it ate at him.

He was angry and grew angrier. He drank even more, chasing the long evenings with Benzedrine in the afternoons. "I will never do this again," he said on the morning that he disappeared. He had scheduled an appointment with a labor organizer, and before he left he took a swig of Teacher's from the bottle that hung from the window on a string. He thought I hadn't noticed.

He vanished, as they put it, "without a trace." A few items about the disappearance of Milo Fitzgerald appeared in the local paper, but they, too, vanished in a few days, and from that point onward I was nothing if not conscious of the gap between the life I knew, and the life the world acknowledged.

Which is why, of course, I looked for my father in *The Book of the Unknown Dead* that day. Had he been one of the hobos? The man who had jumped? The one in the back of the limo?

"But I never finished," I say.

"Why not?"

"Curphey called."

He was in his lab coat, pipe in his mouth, paging through a manila folder and talking on the black telephone when I walked in. He looked up, narrowed his eyes, and said, "May I call you right back?" He hung up and nodded at me. "Sit down, Ben."

I did.

"I've been thinking a lot about you."

"You have?"

"What you said about the diary."

"What about it?"

"You said it was in the Monroe home. But Captain Hamilton sent his men to her home and found nothing."

Captain Hamilton.

"You didn't take it, did you?"

I lied: "No."

"Where is it?"

I said nothing.

"Look, I understand the pressures here, Ben. Really. Which is why you should relax. You *deserve* to. You haven't had a break in quite a while."

"It's been busy."

"I know. But a man has to live. A man has to take care of himself. I worry that you're not." He slid an envelope emblazoned with the LACCO logo across the desk.

"Open it."

I did: It contained one round-trip TWA ticket to Cleveland.

"Cleveland?"

"I want you to go on vacation, and not think about your job. And not worry about Marilyn Monroe. So we've arranged for you to spend some time in Cleveland. At the Pick-Carter. You heard of it?"

"I've hardly even heard of Cleveland."

"It's a lovely hotel. You can only do your job when you're thinking clearly."

"I'm thinking clearly."

"Oh?"

"You don't believe me."

A voice at the door: "Dr. Curphey?"

He looked up. "Yes?"

His secretary. "May I see you for a second, please."

Curphey looked at me as he left the office.

I tapped my finger on his desk and looked around, at the window, the TV, the golf clubs . . . and the bookshelf:

Volumes of history, psychology, forensics . . . and *The Enemy Within* by Robert Kennedy.

Bingo.

I took the book down from the shelf and opened it.

"Dear Dr. Curphey," read the inscription on the inside plate: "With thanks and gratitude. Yours ever, Bobby."

24.

I was on the second floor of the library on Fifth, reading *The Enemy Within* by the green light of a lawyer's lamp on a long oak table. The Monroe diary sat to my right. It was late, I didn't know what time, and I was alone except for the bum who slept with his head on crossed arms two tables ahead. He kept moving in his sleep, snake-like. A severe librarian sat behind the desk in the middle of the room.

I lit a cigarette. I dragged and tried to tamp the ash, but there was no ashtray. I set the butt on the edge of the desk and returned to the book.

In 1955, Robert Kennedy was chairman of the Senate Select Committee on Improper Activities in the Labor or Management Field, also known as the McClellan Committee. Senator John McClellan, D-Arkansas, was chairman. The investigation into Teamster president Dave Beck and, later, Jimmy Hoffa began when the subcommittee started nosing into mob and Teamster involvement in the manufacturing and distribution of clothes for the military.

The dues and savings of the Teamsters were being used by Teamster leaders, President Beck in particular, to buy homes, racehorses, Sulka robes, "twenty-one pairs of nylons, outboard motors, shirts, chairs, love seats, rugs, a gravy boat, a biscuit box, a 20-foot deep freeze, two aluminum boats, a gun, a bow tie, six pairs of knee drawers." The money was also being loaned to people like Morris "Moe" Dalitz, former member of Detroit's Purple Gang, who used it to build the Desert Inn and Stardust Hotel in Las Vegas.

Robert Kennedy, crusader, crossed the country in search of more information. His first stop: Los Angeles. His first contact: Captain James Hamilton of L.A.'s Intelligence Division.

Kennedy met Hamilton and Lieutenant Joseph Stephens, chief of the Police Labor Squad, on November 14, 1956. He talked to members of the Sailors Union of the Pacific. He talked to Anthony Doria, mobster Johnny Dio's friend. He heard about members of the Retail Clerks of San Diego who had been beaten by goons. He heard about the hoods who had tried to take over the L.A. Union of Plumbers and Steamfitters.

There were unsolved murders, bodies in barrels, and the story of the L.A. union organizer who had been told to "stay out of San Diego." Messages on cocktail napkins: "Stay out of San Diego." Phone calls: "No San Diego or you die."

But the man went to San Diego. He intended to organize jukebox operators. He stayed at the Beachcomber Motel. And one night, after a few drinks at the bar, he was ambushed on the way back to his room. Knocked on the back of the head with a blackjack. When he woke, he was lying on Black's Beach. A seagull pecked at his head, blood on its beak. He sat up, waved the birds away—and that was when he felt the pain in his backside.

He wanted to get out of San Diego. He never should have gone to San Diego. But the pain was so bad that he couldn't drive. He called the ambulance. At the hospital, they removed a cucumber from his rectum. It still had a price sticker on it. Back in his car, at the hotel, a note on the passenger seat read:

"Next time it will be a watermelon."

I put the book down and went in search of timelines and logistics. I combed through the last few copies of the *L.A. Times*, tracking the Kennedys' whereabouts from August 4 to yesterday.

And this is what I found:

Bobby had been scheduled to speak at the American Bar Association Conference on Monday, August 6, so he spent the weekend with Ethel and kids at the Bates Ranch in Gilroy, three hundred miles northwest of Los Angeles. On Saturday, Marilyn's last day, everyone went horseback riding.

On Sunday, Bobby attended mass at 9:30 A.M. in Gilroy. "He was without his usual flashy smile and shook hands woodenly with those that welcomed him," one paper said. "Perhaps the cares of the administration are weighing heavily on him."

Perhaps.

I also found this from Dorothy Kilgallen's column in the *New York Journal American*:

> Marilyn Monroe's health must be improving. She's been attending select Hollywood parties and has become the talk of the town again. In California, they're circulating a photograph of her that certainly isn't as bare as the famous calendar, but is very interesting. And she's cooking in the sex-appeal department, too; she's proved vastly alluring to a handsome gentleman who is a bigger name than Joe DiMaggio in his prime. So don't write off Marilyn Monroe as finished.

I felt a tap on my shoulder. The librarian stood above me, wiry gray hair and granny glasses. Dark suit. "Sir," she said.

"Yes."

"You can't smoke in here."

"I wondered why there were no ashtrays."

"Anyway, we're closed," she said, checking her wrist with one swift gesture. She had a little mustache. "It's ten P.M."

"I didn't notice the time. I've been reading."

"And smoking. We're closing."

"I need to use the men's room."

She told me where it was. I picked up the Monroe diary and noticed, as I stood, that the homeless man's right wrist had slipped from his black coat. On it: an expensive wristwatch.

The bathroom door was ajar. The light would not turn on. I heard dripping in the darkness and touched things I didn't want to touch as I made my way to what I hoped were the urinals.

I flushed and stepped back outside.

I walked into Zoology and, through the parallel stacks, saw the homeless man going methodically through my briefcase. He was lifting it up by the handle, shaking out the papers inside, then bending to the floor.

It didn't take a rocket scientist to realize he was looking for the diary. They were *all* looking for it. I was carrying it, nervous: What would they do to get it? I paged to the entries I had not yet read and ripped out as much as I could. I shoved them into the back of my trousers, slipped *The Book of Secrets* between *The Vertebrate Body* and *The World of Plankton*, and walked toward the front room.

The man was gone.

So was my briefcase.

25.

The tavern on Melrose was near the blue tamale place. It was called Joe's. And, no, since you ask, I *don't* remember seeing a flash when I left the car. I figured I was being followed, but I never saw anyone on the sidewalk, with or without a camera. I never saw anyone across the street—at least not at first. The tavern had a sort of stucco, almost adobe, wall. That much I remember. And red neon in dark windows. That's what you can see in the first of the photos they took of me, the photo you have here, Doctor, in the stack of evidence:

> 4. A stained manila folder containing a number of 8 × 10 photographs

In the third photo, taken twenty minutes later, you can see I am leaving the tavern.

It's hard to identify me in the first shot—they did not use a telephoto lens, and the name on the photo reads "Milo," which is not my name.

But in the third shot . . .

"Can I do you for?" the bartender said. Like a bartender in a movie, he had a handlebar mustache and a neat red bow tie and was wiping out the inside of a pint glass with a white towel.

"Wild Turkey, Joe. Neat."

"How'd you know my name is Joe?"

"It's the name on the bar."

"I'm not *that* Joe."

He poured.

I smelled the damp hops. I saw the wood scored with pierced hearts and names of long-ago loves, the black lines from burned cigarettes and damp rings from a century's worth of bottle bottoms. Wet cardboard cases of beer were stacked before the bathroom you could reach just past the pool table. The circular fan set high in the wall at the end of the hall blew out, I somehow knew, into the back of a parking lot where you would find a Dumpster filled with orange rinds and the greasy remains of onion rings and wax paper that had once lined the red plastic baskets.

I lit a cigarette.

"There a phone here?"

"Of course."

There was always a phone. It was set in the dark wall near the front door and the cigarette machine. Inside was a light and a little seat near the dangling phone book.

I called Jo.

The phone, you know, kept ringing. Each ring was followed by a click. The smoke curled and rose to the top of the booth.

"Hello?" A man's metallic voice.

I swallowed. "Jo there?"

"Who's calling?"

I didn't know what to say.

"Who is this?" he said.

I hung up.

I put a dime into the Wurlitzer to the right of the front door and played B-7, "Young World," by the good Ricky Nelson. I didn't care that he was on that TV show people made fun of. He could really tear it up.

I went back to the bar, reached into my pocket, and pulled out the pages I had torn from the diary.

You had to put the pieces together. The writing wasn't always legible. There were random scrawled words and names, like "HORSE BOOK OPEN" and "Roberta Linn." Much of it did not make sense, but the stuff that *did* make sense made clear that, the weekend before Marilyn died, she had gone out to the place that Sinatra owned, a place half in California and half in Nevada, hence its name: Cal-Neva Lodge.

The Nevada half featured gambling. You stepped past the exact geographical point where the states changed in the hall and found yourself in a casino once frequented by the likes of Charles Lindbergh, F. Scott Fitzgerald, Clara Bow, and William Randolph Hearst.

On the weekend of July 28 and 29, Sinatra was performing in the Celebrity Showroom. He'd invited Marilyn to come, she wrote, "just for kicks." But it wasn't kicks. She had taken a lot of pills. She wrote about taking them as Sinatra sang "September Song" and there was champagne and vodka as the room blurred and music faded and she looked up to see a chandelier and ceiling tiles falling from the rain the night before. The tiles were falling on her. She was certain. And one tile became two. And three. Until—

Now there was a flash from the street outside: lightning? No.

A camera?

I carried the pages to the front door and looked out.

Duane Mikkelson, the guy from the *Mirror*, was taking pictures through the window on the sidewalk. He had the same Chiclet teeth that I remembered, crammed into the same gums that were too high when he smiled. The same sunglasses, even at night; the same fedora with the same press pass in it.

I carried the pages past the pool table into the bathroom.

It was dim and green, like an aquarium but without water. No windows.

I locked the door. There was one stall. The toilet inside hadn't been flushed since Grant took Richmond. I shut the cover and stood on it, reaching up for the ceiling tiles. They were all square-shaped and mostly stained with water that had turned yellow. I pushed one up, slid it over, pushed the pages I had ripped on top of another tile inside, then pulled the first tile back over the space.

Dust filtered down. I coughed, wiped my hands against my pants, and jumped off the toilet.

Back at the bar, I saw another flash.

"It's this one, see, Doc?" I point to the second picture in the file. "It's closer; you can see me better, though the name on the photo here is, again, 'Milo.' "

In the third picture, I am standing outside and staring toward the camera, holding my hands above my eyes like an admiral. What you can't see is the car—my car—below the lens. The windows had been shattered, the doors opened, and the seats slit with razors.

My empty, torn briefcase sat on the front seat.

Enter *that* into evidence, Doc.

"It isn't evidence," you say.

"Oh?"

I stepped over the shattered glass, slipped onto the car seat, put the key in the ignition.

But the Rambler didn't start.

I heard thunder. I looked back to the bar and, through the drops on the window, saw the bartender at the door.

And that was when the cab pulled up.

26.

"Weather we're having," the driver said over the sound of the wind wings.

"Sure enough."

"Santa Anas, you know."

"I know."

"The devil's wind, what they call them. What is that phrase? An ill wind blows no good."

"I don't know."

"Sorry? Can't hear you. Gotta speak up."

"I said I don't know! I wouldn't know."

"Wouldn't want weather like this to continue."

"No, sir."

"Coyotes come down from the mountains. They say the other day a woman gave birth to a lion. *Or* a prince."

"You don't say."

"Mud slides and all that. One day it will all just continue, you know. The fires will start and not stop. They say that. It's the end times. Like the Whore of Babylon. The woman who died. The actress. What's her name?"

"Marilyn Monroe."

"Oh, sure. You a churchgoing man?"

"Not exactly."

"Oh, no? Well, it's all in the Bible. You don't live in the mountains, do you?"

"I told you. I live on Wilshire."

"Oh, sure. By the big hotel."

"Yeah. That."

"Up-and-coming neighborhood, I heard."

"More or less. The place is smoky, though. And old."

"Oh, that can't be good."

"No."

"Can't be good for you, I mean," he said. "Or your son."

"Well, I'm trying to—" I started to say *save up enough money to move.* But I stopped, of course. "How did you know that I have a son?"

I saw his eyes in the rearview mirror. I thought I saw his mouth, too, smiling. But that must be a memory that I applied later, because I could not have seen his mouth. Not in the rearview mirror. I saw his eyes, though, in the light from a passing car as we drove onto a deserted road.

"You told me you had a son," he said.

"I didn't."

"Of course you did. How else would I know?"

"That's my question."

"And my answer is: You told me."

The lights were dying behind us. "Where are we going?"

"To your hotel."

"I don't know where we are."

The radio was filled with static. It was tuned to a talk show featuring a man playing muted music and speaking in a throaty voice: "Whatever happened to 'Good night, stars, I love you'? Or whatever happened to 'Starlight, star bright, first star I see tonight'? Whatever happened to Jack Armstrong, the All-American boy? As the aging hand of time runs her fingers through my hair, all I can think of is: Whatever happened to 'Now I lay me down to sleep, I pray the Lord my soul to keep'?"

The driver adjusted the knob, the passing stations fuzzy and crackling. Here and there he got a signal:

"—live, coming to you from the world-famous Cocoanut Grove where—"

"—on the floor of the bathroom as the children—"

"—cruise with a throng of the other Kennedy clansmen Sunday and then a bit of solitude, just the president and Mrs. Kennedy, before they part today."

We were moving through the hills, lightning in the clouds. I figured we were taking the back roads around 101, what locals call Freeway 101, following the old thoroughfare that linked the Spanish missions. The roads are mostly rural, black stretches heading into a midnight broken only by abandoned hotels and railroad quarries and gas stations lit by Coke machines. There weren't any cars, and though for maybe twenty minutes I contemplated pulling on the handle and jumping into the night, we were speeding, and a roll across that pavement would have killed me.

We finally pulled up a winding muddy canyon road. The words TRIPLE XXX RANCH were set in dead neon on the arched entrance.

"Right," the driver said, parking just under the sign. The wings went back and forth. "That'll be five sixty."

"This isn't my building."

His eyes lifted in the mirror. "You asked me to drive you. I drove you. It's a simple transaction: You owe me five sixty."

"I'm not paying you for leaving me out in the middle of nowhere."

"I have ways of dealing with deadbeats."

He pushed his palm against the padded horn.

Headlights from another car flashed through the rain on the windshield.

Someone opened the cab's back door, and I was yanked into the mud, staring up at a man with a psychopathically grinning Jimmy Cagney face and a porkpie hat as the cab pulled away, rolling through the arches.

"You're supposed to be on vacation," the man said. He was short and wiry, like an Irish boxer. "Why aren't you on vacation?"

"I got bored."

"Where is *The Book of Secrets*?"

Rain fell like a veil around his head.

"I don't know what—"

There were other men. I hadn't seen them at first, but now they were behind me. One of them picked me up, both hands under my armpits, and held me close to his hard heavy chest as the small man in the hat hauled off and punched me in the jaw.

The night went white, my head rocking back. I blinked, lips drooling blood and rain, and stared at him. The headlights blinded me. He was a black shadow surrounded by light.

"I'm not going to ask you again," he said. "Where is *The Book of Secrets*?"

"I don't know."

He punched me again. Harder, this time. My head jolted back. I heard a crack. I saw stars. I saw more stars than were in the heavens. Or MGM. The second man tightened his grip as Cagney reached into his jacket pocket, LAPD shield flashing, and pulled out a cucumber.

"It's in the library," I said.

27.

Ben."

I took the ice pack off my face and opened my eyes. As much as I could. They were bloody slits, but I could see Jo.

She stood above me as I lay on a gurney near a moaning guy on yet another gurney just two feet away. She was dressed, as always, like Edith Head. She wore a clean-lined bias-cut cream dress with oversized pink buttons. (Don't ask me how I know all this.) She wore jet earrings, too. At her sides, like matching luggage, sat a bag from I. Magnin and her purse.

"Jo."

"Shh!"

"What time is it?"

"Eleven or so."

"That means nothing to me. Why are you here?"

"Hospital called."

"Why?"

"You put me down as next of kin."

"What?"

"They asked for next of kin, and you said me."

"Must have been delirious."

"Oh, I don't know," she said. "I'm touched."

"Yeah, well, I was touched myself about a hundred times tonight, and right now I'm not feeling so great."

"They said blunt trauma to the face and chest. A fractured rib and nasal fractures. And echees . . ."

"Ecchymoses."

"What's that?"

"Bruises. They tried to put a cucumber up my ass."

"Jesus, you poor kid."

"I'm not a kid."

"You are to me. I'm old enough to be your mother."

"Sure, if you reached sexual maturity at five."

"I was very advanced for my age," she said. "Can I smoke in here?"

"If *he* doesn't mind." I tilted my head in the direction of the guy on the gurney next to mine. "Do you mind, mister?" I said. "If she smokes?"

He merely groaned.

There was a red prayer candle under his gurney. It was technically illegal, a fire hazard, but this was a Catholic hospital, so what's illegal?

"Now." Jo lit a cigarette. "What happened?"

"They beat me up."

"I can see that. Who's they?"

"What do you get when you cross an elephant with a rhinoceros?"

"What?"

"Hell-if-I-know," I said, and told her everything: the B. F. Fox van, the intruder in the Savoy with a work order for nonexistent work, done by a nonexistent company at a nonexistent address, and ending when I told them where the diary was. As I spoke, she wrote in her reporter's notebook, quickly slipped from her purse.

Ah, so this was no mere social call.

"How did you get *here*?" she asked.

"I woke on the grounds of the Triple XXX Ranch, and the next thing I knew . . ."

I was at a liquor store along the service road. The rain had stopped, leaving puddles in the lot. The neon sign above the door buzzed like an insect, the I missing from LIQUORS.

A bell rang overhead when I stepped into the fluorescence. A man stood on the ladder to the right, stocking shelves above refrigerator cases in his overalls. A woman sat on a swivel chair behind the counter covered with cigar boxes and small racks of sexual aids. On the shelf behind her, "nature" magazines were wrapped in brown paper. The cigarette dropped from the woman's lips when she saw my bloody clothes and face.

She opened her mouth, as if to scream, but "It's okay," I said. "I need a cab."

"I'm calling the police!"

"Please." I took my wallet from the pocket of my bloody pants and tried to hand her money, but all I found was the Get Out of Jail Free card.

Thirty minutes later, the paramedic in the back of the ambulance was leaning over me, saying, "Do you know your name?"

"Ben Fitzgerald."

"Do you know where you are, Mr. Fitzgerald?"

"In the back of an ambulance."

"What happened, Mr. Fitzgerald?"

"I took a cab."

"He's delirious."

At the hospital, the resident injected me with morphine and packed my nose to stop the bleeding and applied the cold compress.

And the next thing I knew I opened my eyes to find Jo looking like Vivien Leigh. Dressed like Edith Head. With her bag from I. Magnin.

I. Magnin was where she bought most of her clothes. That and Bullock's on Wilshire. But the clothes inside this particular bag were men's clothes, nice ones: Sulka underwear, socks, a silk undershirt, a Van Heusen shirt, a striped tie, high-rising slip-on Bond Street shoes with square toes and wingtips, and a chocolate-brown worsted pin-striped suit.

"A suit."

"It's brown for town," she said. "With black stripings, see?"

"Sure."

"Now let's get you into some respectable drawers."

"I'm not supposed to put on underwear, Jo. I'm in a hospital gown."

"I wouldn't be caught *dead* in a hospital gown."

"So you'll die at home."

"With dignity—and stiletto heels. Come on." She held the underwear up. "It's lovely. Sulka makes such a*dor*able vicuña dressing gowns."

"You know you have a tendency to overemphasize certain syllables in words? Webster is turning over in his grave."

"Webster never wore Sulka. Go on: I won't look."

She dropped her cigarette to the floor, crushed it with her heel, and handed me the pair of briefs.

I had some trouble slipping them on under the hospital gown. She helped by lifting my legs.

"No fair," I said, adjusting the briefs. "You peeked."

"I didn't have much choice," she said. "Did anyone ever tell you that you have a great ass?"

"No."

"With or without the cucumber. You could bounce a quarter off that ass."

"Wouldn't you rather buy a Clark bar?"

She leaned over and kissed my forehead.

"Hey, that's nice," I said.

She kissed me again: this time, on the mouth.

"You shouldn't do that."

"Why not?"

"Makes my head hurt."

"That's what morphine is for."

"Morphine doesn't work for that kind of hurt."

"Maybe this will." She took a pint of Canadian Club from her purse. "I figured you could use it."

"Just don't let the nurses see."

She cracked the seal and looked around. She frowned. "This is awfully familiar."

"What?"

"No water glass."

"The service here is awful," I said. "Waitress!"

Jo put her left forefinger on my lips. "Shh!"

"Nurse!"

The nurse arrived. "Mr. Fitzgerald?"

Jo spun around, shoving the bottle into her purse.

"May we have a water glass, ma'am? Make that two?"

"Mr. Fitzgerald." The nurse did not move. "I'll have you know that this is not a restaurant."

"No wonder the food is so bad."

But the whiskey was good. It helped all kinds of hurt. Jo sat on the edge of the gurney, and we drank it straight from the bottle, since the Evil Nurse never returned. Jo passed it to me, and I passed it to her as I told her that Bobby Kennedy was "the enemy within."

"Well, of course!" Her eyes widened. "That's it! The diary is about Bobby. Well, it's right there: She called him the General. He was the *attorney* general, and he wore white socks with a black suit, and he was the 'altar boy,' the mama's boy. Which is what Bobby is. Or was."

"It just seems odd."

"What?"

"The attorney general of the United States was fucking Marilyn Monroe? Seriously?"

"I'll take that and raise you twenty: The *president* of the United States was fucking Marilyn Monroe."

"Ridiculous."

"Why?"

"He's the president of the United States."

"So that makes him perfect? He has a cock."

"*I* have a cock."

"I noticed."

"Not all men are cheaters, Jo."

"Oh? And you?"

"The heart of all morality is staying out of certain rooms."

"You were caught in a woman's hotel room."

"I was drunk."

"That's an excuse? Tell that to the Kennedys."

"I believe in the New Frontier."

"The New Frontier is hooey, Ben, like everything else about the guy: It's public relations, advertising. They sold Jack into that job the way they'd sell soap. Joe Kennedy said this, in an interview. You think that guy believes in what he's selling? JFK has been packaged for your consumption. You think he's not cheating on Jackie? When he was elected, one of his aides said, 'This administration is going to do for sex what the last one did for golf.'"

Jo said that Kennedy had carried on an "illicit relationship with another man's wife" during World War II and [redacted] with a woman in Las Vegas. He dated a woman named Inga Arvad, who'd attended the 1936 Summer Olympics with Hitler. He dated a woman named Judith Exner, who was also dating Mafia chieftain Sam Giancana. There were others, too—so many that Jack could never remember their names. "Kid" was what he called them. "Hello, kid," he once told a woman in his hotel during the 1960 campaign. "We have only fifteen minutes."

Fifteen minutes was all he ever needed.

"And then," Jo said, "there was Florence."

"Who?"

"Florence M. Kater. You never heard of her?"

"No."

She handed me the bottle and said, "Drink."

28.

She was a housewife who had rented a room in her Georgetown duplex to a woman named Pamela Turnure, an aide in the office of the young, ambitious Massachusetts senator John F. Kennedy. The elegant, lovely, and poised Miss Turnure seemed the very model of the perfect tenant, but Mrs. Florence Kater soon became annoyed by the young woman's behavior. Mrs. Kater had, as she'd told her own husband, Marty, clearly and repeatedly stipulated that her tenant keep "regular hours" and be "quiet." The hours the lovely Miss Turnure kept, however, were anything but regular, the time she spent in her small apartment at the top of the stairs anything but quiet, her behavior more befitting a barmaid than what Mrs. Kater would have called a "lady."

It turned out that the elegant Miss Turnure was making what Mrs. Kater called "violent love" in the upstairs bedroom, just down the hall past the staircase from Mrs. Kater and her husband. And when, annoyed, one night, by the fifth successive incident of "violent noise" from the "banging" of the bed and what she called "male mooing like an ox," Mrs. Kater sat up in bed next to Marty, who asked what was wrong.

"It's that woman again," she said.

"What woman?"

"The Turnure woman! Don't you hear it?"

"Go back to sleep, Mother."

"But just *hear* it," she said. "There's a man in the house."

"So she has a boyfriend."

"It's against the rules," Mrs. Kater said.

She was a short woman whose auburn hair had begun to gray but was dyed and styled every week under the UFO-like hair dryers by Darlene, the single mom, at the beauty shop down the street. She wore pillbox hats and pearls and her hair surrounded the moon of her face in a fiery corona of Aqua Net. She was a woman of convictions that were sealed in the chamber of her heart where nothing could touch them. She liked rules, order, straight lines, neat answers, final decisions. She was a certain person who believed in certainty.

She was certain that her tenant was lying to her. She found her scuffed slippers near the bed with her toes, wrapped the bathrobe that hung on the bedpost around her faintly shivering body, and walked, still wearing her cap and curlers, to the tenant's door and knocked.

She heard giggling. Shushing. Then nothing.

She knocked again: "What are you doing in there?"

"Decorating," Miss Turnure said.

"I hear a man in there. No men are allowed in here."

"I'm moving furniture."

"I am trying to sleep. Please keep the noise down."

A muffled "sorry," followed by more giggling.

But Mrs. Kater was awake. She had never been a good sleeper. Sleep was even harder to come by now that she was older. There were pills by her bed but they made her feel groggy in the morning.

The male mooing continued. The banging continued. *Some decorating!* Mrs. Kater thought, wide awake and furious now in bed. It was (she later recalled) 1:16 A.M. when, deciding to catch her pretty tenant in a lie, she went down to the parlor with a bay window overlooking Hope near the river and waited with her legs crossed under the bathrobe in the light from over the road. She waited almost without moving until, at 1:35, the door creaked upstairs; she heard more shushing and giggling as the yellow light spread onto the wall and floor. And into the light stepped a handsome young man with his shoes.

He held them twinned in his left hand as his right palm grazed the banister. He tiptoed down the stairs, rocking exaggeratedly back and forth, his head lowered as if wanting to know exactly what his feet were doing. Mrs. Kater, never reticent, marched across the floor to the carpet at the base of the stairs and stared straight into the face of the man who looked, surprised, at the fierce little woman in curlers.

"It was Senator Kennedy," Mrs. Kater said later in the only interview she ever gave. "Senator *Jack* Kennedy. He gave me that smile that he gives everyone and held out the right hand that he holds out to everyone and said what I suppose seemed the right thing to say at the time, which was, 'Good evening, ma'am.' "

"It isn't evening," Mrs. Kater said. "It's *morning*. And you have woken me for the fifth time in a row. And for the last time! You with your male mooing like an ox."

"I don't moo."

"You mooed."

She did not care who this young man was, or how much money his family had, or how powerful his father was, or how far he was going. She did not care who he would become or what it might mean to the country or the world. He was the unwanted guest of a female tenant who had broken Mrs. Kater's stated rules. The rules were quite clear and they were firm. The rules, however, had been ignored and this was "cause," Mrs. Kater announced, "for eviction. I will," she said, "evict her."

Kennedy then showed the arrogance—what the Mob called *hamartia*—that was, despite his charm, the mark of the beast on his family. "Ma'am," he said, "I don't care what the fuck you do."

And with that he left the house and the sleepless housewife behind. She watched him walk, shoes in hand, his untucked white shirt trailing like a duck's behind, across the street.

Now, Mrs. Kater was not timid. She was not a woman to be, as she called it, "deterred." She was mad now. Her tenant, a guest who had broken the rules and who did not seem to care, was "making violent love"—Mrs. Kater's words—to the famous senator from Boston. A man who in the darkness of her own living room, carrying his shoes, had said "fuck" to her. To her! Mrs. Florence Kater! Well, she would not sit "idly by," she said, while two good-looking young people kept her up all night on account of what she called "rutting." Who did they think she was? Well, she was Mrs. Florence Kater.

And she had a plan.

She found the Kodak 44A, 127 roll film camera at Don's Photo on Eighteenth Street. It took twelve pictures a roll, each 44mm square. It was the first camera, Don explained, that featured a plastic lens, but "don't worry," he told Mrs. Kater. "It's very high quality: Perspex."

"What's Perspex?"

"A glass alternative. From Combined Optical Industries."

"I don't care about that," Mrs. Kater said. "Can it take pictures at night?"

"Of course." He pointed to the flash. "See?"

She paid for it, returning to the house near the nice park and the river. She ascended the steps that seemed higher each day and removed the keys from the pouch of the purse where the keys always were and put the bronze in the lock of the door. She was turning the key when she heard the giggling.

Giggling? Like the giggling she had heard last night. And the man's voice. That man! *That man!* The senator was back!

She opened the door and stepped into the living room.

Her husband!

Her husband stood, grinning and (she noticed) beltless, before the swivel chair on which the lovely Turnure sat with legs extended, as if applying nail polish, revealing panties beneath her short skirt. She wore hose that made her legs look, as the French say, "more nude than nude," and she gazed girlishly up at Marty (her husband!) as he lazily slapped the bottoms of her bare feet with the flyswatter.

It wasn't even summer!

"Shoo," Miss Turnure was saying as Mrs. Kater stepped in. "Shoo, fly."

"Marty!"

Marty spun and Miss Turnure looked up, the mirth in their eyes dying. Marty lowered the flyswatter, comically raised as if to strike the lovely Miss Turnure. His lower lip protruded. Lovely Miss Turnure herself lowered her pink feet to the floor. They pressed firmly against the wood—but, Mrs. Kater noticed, her toes wiggled luxuriously.

"Hello, Mother," Marty said.

"Don't call me that. For godssakes, Marty: What are you doing?"

"Killing flies."

"On Miss Turnure's *feet*? Dear God!"

That night a siren sounded through the window. Martin, a heavy sleeper, had sunk to bed like a sack of cement and was snoring. He had been snoring since midnight. Mrs. Kater, on the other hand, was awake and staring at the ceiling. Waiting.

She sighed. The Kodak 44A was under the bed, loaded with film. At 1:25, she thought she heard the door open downstairs. She sat up. She was wearing curlers under a plastic hairnet; white cold cream covered her face. Her ears twitched like a fox's.

She heard the creak of wood and footsteps on the floorboards as someone walked through the living room. She heard the same feet climb the steps. She stood and walked across her own floor to the door that was open partway. She peered through it and watched as Senator Kennedy, D-Mass., crept with shoes again in his hand to the door across the hallway.

A light came from under the Turnure woman's door. The senator opened the door, and for a second she saw rosy Pamela standing nude against the light from inside. She was smiling. She giggled softly, then opened the door, exposing her pink breasts, taking the senator into her arms.

They shut the door.

Mrs. Kater swallowed.

It wouldn't be long now.

It never was.

She walked to Marty in the darkness. "Marty," she whispered, shoving him with her hands. "It's them again."

"Wha," he muttered, still snoring.

"It's happening again."

"Go back to sleep."

But of course she could not, and knowing that she only had a few minutes left, she retrieved the camera from under the bed and tiptoed down the stairs to the front of the house and saw that the senator, D-Mass., had left the front door unlocked. More villainy! More treachery! For all she knew, half of the night street was now inside her home!

She walked outside, shutting the door behind her, and waited in the bushes to the right of the front door, camera in hand.

The picture that she finally took," Jo said, "showed Senator John F. Kennedy emerging from the front door of the Kater brownstone in Georgetown with his shoes in his hand. Mrs. Florence M. Kater sent it to thirty-two journalists. Myself included. She also sent it to the FIBS."

"The Fibs."

"The FBI. She was almost unhinged. Her sense of justice, sense of religion as a Catholic—all of these things were 'grievously wounded.' That's what she said in her letter. She was a nut but what bugged her about Mr. D-Mass. was that he had lied. He claimed to have principles but he'd lied. He didn't give a shit. He only cared about himself and his success. And Mrs. Florence Kater wanted the world to know the truth."

"So what happened to the photographs?"

"That's the whole point: nothing."

"Nothing."

"Blackout. Shutdown. Nothing. Every journalist I knew went to their editors. And their editors went to the publishers. The photo of Senator Kennedy went all the way up the food chain. And that's where it vanished. No one would touch it. Not with that proverbial ten-foot pole. Mrs. Kater checked the papers every morning. And not just the *Washington Post*. She checked every paper she'd sent the picture to, and not one reported the story. She couldn't understand it. She was sure something had gone wrong. She made phone calls. No one called her back. She made appointments. They were canceled. The world was closing off. And then her house was robbed, her precious jewelry stolen. But what really galled her, what offended her in the deepest part of her being, and down to her core, was the fact that when she returned to the bedroom after snapping Kennedy, that night, she had seen Marty's hand moving frantically under the bedcovers.

"He was masturbating," Jo said, and leaned down to kiss me.

29.

"Jo."

"Shh!"

"The nurse."

"Fuck her."

"Guy over there."

"Is so doped up he won't remember in the morning."

She was kissing me again, leaning over the gurney when I said, "Jo?"

"Mmm."

"Who answered your phone?"

"What?"

"I called you earlier. A man answered."

"Oh, that was *you*," she said. "My father."

"Your father."

"I take care of him sometimes."

A voice: "What are you doing?"

I looked up.

It was the nurse.

"I'm just searching for some marbles," Jo said, standing. She brushed the waist of her dress, and turned to me: "I didn't see any Greenies, did you?"

"No."

"I'm getting a bad feeling about this," the nurse said. "And you were smoking! I can tell you were smoking!"

"It's *that*." Jo pointed to the votive burning under the nearby gurney. "The candles aren't exactly up to code, are they?"

"*God* is the code."

"God isn't the fire department."

The man groaned.

"You, you hussy," the nurse said, "are the whore of Babylon."

"As long as my reputation hasn't reached Beverly Hills."

"May God forgive you."

"I don't care about forgiveness," she said. "I just want my marbles back."

The nurse left in a huff.

We finished the Canadian Club.

"So what does that Florence Kater story mean?" I said.

"It means the Kennedys can do whatever they want. After Kennedy was elected, he made Pamela Turnure Jackie's press secretary, for crying out loud."

"Okay, that's one thing. But you're not really suggesting that JFK and Bobby killed Marilyn Monroe."

"They had motive. She was prepared to go public."

"The brothers weren't anywhere near Los Angeles that night."

"How do you know?"

"It was in the papers."

"Do you always believe what you read?"

"Jack was in Hyannisport. Bobby was in Gilroy. That's three hundred miles away. On Saturday, Bobby went horseback riding. On Sunday, he went to church at nine-thirty. Are you telling me that the attorney general of the United States sort of magically disappeared after horseback riding, flew out to Los Angeles to kill Marilyn, and managed to show up again for church by Sunday morning? It's not possible."

"Then who took off outside Peter Lawford's house?"

"I don't know what you're talking about."

"Jeanne Carmen said there was a *contretemps* with Lawford's neighbors the night Marilyn died."

"Who's Jeanne Carmen?"

"An actress. Does it matter? She said the neighbors were annoyed by the sand in their pool."

"The sand?"

"The helicopter kicked it up when it left the Lawford property. The neighbors heard the noise. Who was in that helicopter, Ben?"

"It couldn't have been Bobby Kennedy."

"Well, it sure as hell wasn't Irving Berlin," she said. "Inga Arvad was a Nazi. Judith Exner was a mob moll. And all that got swept under the rug. Why was Marilyn any different?"

"Because she was a movie star?"

"That's not what Jeanne said. She said it wasn't about sex," Jo said. "It was something much more scandalous."

"What's more scandalous than sex?"

"Politics," she said.

WEDNESDAY, AUGUST 8

30.

I saw the funeral on TV. I was lying in the hospital room on the fifth floor staring up into the set that was bolted to the wall and tilting toward me. My head was propped on two pillows; tubes were in my nose, a hep-lock IV drip taped to my arm.

"The curtain falls," the TV anchor said into the camera. He stood before the wall that separated the mortuary grounds from the street and all the staring people. "Brief and simple are the rites that mark the funeral of Marilyn Monroe. We grasp at straws, as if knowing how she died—or why—might enable us to bring her back . . ."

They showed Westwood Village, where the funeral would be held. The sign looked cheap, like a roadside attraction, a small "Swiss" hotel along some unused highway:

WESTWOOD VILLAGE

MEMORIAL PARK AND MORTUARY

Forty men with walkie-talkies stood outside.

People shouted and took pictures.

According to the *Times*, "special police from movie studios" and "agents of the Pinkerton Detective Agency" would be inside. Monroe would be wearing her wig from *The Misfits* and a chartreuse dress she'd purchased in Florence. No jewelry. A solid bronze casket would be lined with champagne-colored velvet.

The Suicide Squad was "still active," the *Times* said, quoting Tabachnick saying they had talked to doctors in the case and friends of the dead actress. It quoted Farberow saying that it may be "another two weeks" before Curphey's office reached a "final decision."

Arthur Miller said he did not think she had taken her own life. Publicist Pat Newcomb said the same, adding that she had made plans: On Monday, Marilyn had an appointment with her lawyer. On Tuesday she was scheduled to meet with J. Lee Thompson, producer of *The Guns of Navarone*. On September 12, she was scheduled to be in New York for an *Esquire* cover shoot.

Suicide, the paper said, ranks as the ninth cause of death in California.

Every morning, the week that followed, they woke me at four-thirty so that one of the residents could take my temperature and blood pressure. Why these tests seemed more important than sleep, I have no idea—especially since they kept telling me to "get some rest."

I got so little. Partly because of the noises in the place, but mostly because I didn't stop thinking about what Jo had said about the sand in the pool near the Lawford house. On the day I was released, I asked for a Yellow Pages and paged through the H's to "Helicopter."

There were four helicopter companies in Los Angeles but only one in Santa Monica. That was Conners on Clover Field. It was a fifteen-acre landing site named for World War I pilot Lieutenant Greayer "Grubby" Clover. It was the home of Douglas Aircraft, which had moved to an abandoned movie studio in 1922 and started making military planes. They tested them on Clover Field.

During World War II, Douglas realized that their plant was vulnerable to air attack, so they worked with a team of Warner Brothers set designers to camouflage it. They stretched five million square feet of chicken wire over four hundred poles, covering the terminal, hangars, and parking lots. On top of this, they built fake wood-frame houses complete with garages, fences, clotheslines—and even "trees" made of the same chicken wire. They spray-painted chicken feathers to look like leaves, then covered the runway with green paint and turned the largest hangar into a hill.

The place was so well disguised that even the pilots who knew about it had trouble finding it, and when the camouflage was eliminated, in 1945, the neighbors mourned as if a monument had been torn down.

I picked up the telephone and called Conners.

A man answered. "Hello?"

Did I really want to do this? Was it worth it? Jack Clemmons was in Italy. The doctors were in the Côte d'Azur. Eunice Murray was God only knew where, along with Pat Newcomb. They had all disappeared, leaving me the last man standing, but what price would I pay for the truth?

I hung up.

At 2:15, I put on the clothes that Jo had brought.

A monogram had been stitched in red above the left pocket of the new shirt:

JEH, it read.

WEDNESDAY, AUGUST 15

31.

I wasn't thinking about Marilyn and wouldn't think of Marilyn and the only reason I went back to Joe's on Melrose was to get my ruined car. I didn't intend to walk inside the place, and I wouldn't have walked inside the place—except for the fact that I couldn't find a pay phone on the sidewalk.

Joe was mopping up the bar as I walked to the bank of lit phones to the right of the door. I sat on the stool under a phone and put a dime in and called a tow truck.

"Be right there."

I hung up.

I would not think of the diary. I wasn't thinking of the diary as I played "Young World" on the Wurlitzer and sat at the bar. I smelled the familiar and comforting smell of damp hops. I saw the wood scored with pierced hearts and long-ago loves, the black lines from burned cigarettes. But I've said this already, haven't I?

I went up to the bar.

"Jesus," Joe said. "What happened to you?"

"Cut myself shaving."

"You and Albert Anastasia."

"Very funny."

"What can I get you?"

"Budweiser."

"Kinda early, isn't it?"

"I had a rough day."

"You look it."

"Gee, thanks."

"Anytime."

I waited for the tow truck. I wasn't thinking about Marilyn. I was on vacation, after all, but after another Budweiser (okay, three), the truck still hadn't arrived and I really had to pee.

Sorry for the vulgarity.

"No problem," you say.

I stood from the bar with the foam still in the glass and walked past the table to the bathroom. I wasn't going to look for what was left of the diary, but the truth is that I didn't use the urinal. I used a stall—the same stall, in fact, where I had hidden the torn pages.

I was whistling and pissing when I couldn't help myself: I looked up to see the tile over the toilet slipped just slightly to the right. Past it was darkness, and . . . what?

Pages?

I flushed, closed the cover, stood and pushed the tile over, my head rising from the light into the darkness, eyes above the ceiling line, staring across the tile tops, past rattraps and rusted pipes, searching for the diary.

"It's gone," I said back in the phone booth. "Someone took it, Jo. I came back to get the car, and—"

"Mr. Fitzgerald?" A woman's voice.

"Jo?"

"This ain't Jo." It was Mabel, the colored maid. "Jo ain't here."

"Where is she?"

"That club on Sunset."

The club was Ciro's, the place on the Strip that, like so much else, had devolved from its status as a glamour spot for movie stars to a mostly empty place that was, that evening, as quiet as a chapel mid-week. It *was* mid-week, after all, which meant the only people in the place were serious drinkers, as the blonde who sat like a living doll with Jo at the table in the corner was a serious drinker.

Listen: By living doll, I don't mean that she was beautiful. I mean that she was scary, as a life-sized doll propped in a chair with a highball and fried blond hair would, in fact, be scary. She waved her burning cigarette over the cloudy empty glass, pulpy limes lolling in the melting ice.

Her name was Jeanne Carmen. Now you ask who that is, Doctor; no one knows anymore. I sure as hell didn't. The truth is that you might see her on the *Late Show*. She was the daughter of the lighthouse keeper in *The Monster of Piedras Blancas* and Lillibet in *Untamed Youth*. She is now a trick-shot golfer and a friend of the famous—mostly Marilyn's. They had been, she said, "pill buddies," sharing downers and stories of the men that Jeanne called her "extracurriculars."

As for Jo: She was wearing sporty Capri pants colored with Picasso blurs of greens, reds, oranges, odd browns; that and sugary pink lipstick. She looked like an unfinished art project, but it was Fashion. "What are you doing here?" she asked me.

"I'm looking for you."

"I'm doing an interview."

"I need to talk."

"You look like Don Taylor," Jeanne Carmen said. "Anyone tell you that?"

"No. I'm Ben."

"Jeanne Carmen."

She transferred her cigarette to her left hand and extended her right wrist. It was bent like a fairy's. She wanted me to kiss, not shake, it. So I did. Her whole face puckered in a smile. She smelled of an Eau de Something that only partly masked a deeper smell, that of nicotine and, more, decay.

"Nice to meet you, ma'am," I said. "I don't even know who Don Taylor is."

"He was in *Naked City*. But he wasn't naked. More's the pity. Isn't that what Shakespeare said?"

"He said a lot of things."

"More's the pity. You look like a young Don Taylor. Were you ever a soldier?"

"No."

"Don was, in and out of bed. Lovely boy. Would you like a drink?"

"Wild Turkey, neat."

"Yoo-hoo!" She tried to flag one of the waiters who prowled the damp place like superannuated penguins. They all seemed to have bald heads shiny under strands of unwashed hair and mottled with sunspots so large they looked like continents. "Damn them." She stood and walked across the room to the bar.

I turned to Jo. She was all angles and attitude now, her voice cold and clipped.

"You get out of here, Ben."

"Listen," I said. "I went back to the bar. It's where I hid the extra pages. No one would know they were there, unless—"

"Ben, you're like Bluebird's wife."

"Blue*beard*."

"Whatever. Stop opening that door. You said the heart of all morality is staying out of certain rooms. So clever of you! You're a clever boy. But the heart of all *safety* is staying out of certain rooms, too. Now, stop being Pandora. Stop opening the box."

"*You're* opening it, too."

"I'm a journalist."

"You're Annie Laurie."

"Not if I can help it. Will you listen to me?"

"I'm listening."

"They've threatened you."

"They did more than that."

"They did you a favor: They let you live. But guess what happens next time?"

"It will be a watermelon?"

"There!" Jeanne said, pulling her chair out again and settling back at the table. "That's settled! One Wild Turkey, coming up. Now." Her hand was on my left thigh. "Where were we?"

"I think we're finished," Jo said.

"I was telling you about the tape," she said.

"What tape?" I asked.

Jo said: "*Enough.*"

Jeanne winced against the stream of smoke that rose from her cigarette, frowned with that stained mouth, and stood, gripping the back of her chair. She stared down at me. "You're lovely, Don. Anyone ever tell you that?"

"Only Shakespeare."

"Shut! Up!" she said, and left.

I turned to Jo. "What was *that* all about?"

"I was finished with the interview."

"You were hiding something."

"Or protecting you. Let's get a drink."

"I already did."

"Well, I'm thirsty," she said, trying to flag down the waiter.

"Good luck," I said. "And now about these clothes."

32.

The clothes: I still have the shirt, Doc. It is hanging on the back of the chair that I am sitting in. When you look over my shoulder, I know what you are thinking. I suppose that I can read your mind.

You want to see the shirt.

I stand, take it off the chair, and hand it to you. You feel the fabric in your fingers, then touch the monogram.

"JEH," you say. "Who's that?"

"I didn't know."

"But you know now."

I nod.

"Tell me, Ben: Why did you trust Jo Carnahan?"

"The clothes that you brought me are pretty fancy," I said.

"And you look pretty in them."

"Except they're not mine."

She kept waving for the waiter.

"Jo, someone else's monogram is on this shirt. Whose monogram is it?"

"What," she said, "do you get when you cross an elephant with a rhinoceros?"

"You know the answer to that one."

"I'm sorry. It's embarrassing. I didn't buy them new."

"You didn't."

"I got them secondhand. Over on Melrose. But they're beautiful. That's all that matters. Okay, so I'm not as swell as I'd like you to think."

"Your hands are shaking."

"I never know what to do with my hands," she said. "I need something."

"Light a cigarette."

She did and took a drag, squinted against the smoke, and stared at something over my shoulder. "Wait a second," she said.

"What?"

"Don't turn around until I tell you."

"Why?"

"I said, don't turn around."

I kept staring. She dragged on that cigarette, blowing the smoke out.

"Your hands," I said. "They're—"

"Now."

He was a tall stout man with gray hair that was Brylcreemed and combed in a way that made it look almost plastic. He wore round dark sunglasses and a serge double-breasted bespoke jacket. It was unbuttoned over his gut. His nose was thin and long. He had rings on both hands. He was smoking a cigarette, extending his right pinkie in a way that would have seemed effete if he hadn't seemed so menacing.

That's the word: *menacing.* He had what I later learned was called the Mafia stare: You don't look someone in the eyes. You look at their forehead and don't blink.

"I saw him in the grocery store this morning," Jo said.

"*You* go grocery shopping?"

"Sure."

"You don't strike me as a coupon clipper."

"Who said anything about coupons?"

"Jo, you hardly eat."

"Cigarettes. Will you listen?"

"I'm listening."

"You know how supermarkets have those kind of geometric stacks of canned peas and things? Marvels of engineering the Egyptians might envy?"

"I don't know if the Egyptians—"

"Humor me."

"Okay."

"I passed a stack of canned peas and there he was, holding one of the cans up at me."

"So."

"He asked if I wanted the peas, and I said no. He said the peas were good for you and also delicious. I said I wasn't interested and please leave me alone. I was only looking for cigarettes and maybe some Ovaltine. He said the Ovaltine was in aisle seven. Said I was in the wrong aisle. Well, I wanted to get out, so I went to the checkout and looked behind me. I didn't see him—until I went out to my car."

"Your car."

"He was staring through the window."

Now the man dropped a dime into the jukebox, hit some letter-number combination, and turned toward us as the vinyl spun.

"Young World" began playing.

"Come on," Jo said. "Let's go."

"Where?"

"The Dairy Queen," she said. "Where else?"

33.

The Tall Man followed us from Ciro's, still smoking. He pretended not to see us but stepped to the edge of Sunset and dropped his cigarette.

He was Italian, Doctor.

There was valet parking. The monkey attendant showed up, grabbed Jo's ticket, and ran down the lot to her car. When he pulled back up with Jo's DeSoto, she handed him a dollar and thanked him.

"Come on, darling." She grabbed my hand. "What are you waiting for?"

"My car."

"Shh!"

She pushed me into the driver's side, because of course the *man* would drive, and I fumbled with the stick and looked into the rearview mirror to see the Tall Man staring after us as we pulled into the traffic.

"Hang on," Jo said. "Don't go too fast."

"It's a stick."

"So?"

"I don't know how to drive a stick."

"Why didn't you tell me?"

"You didn't give me the chance."

I was on Cienega when Jo's hands started shaking again.

"It's nothing," she said.

"What?"

"The lights in the car."

"Which?"

"The one behind us."

It was a Ford Fairlane. And not just any Ford Fairlane—it was the one with dice dangling from the rearview mirror. I assumed it belonged to the Man from Ciro's, but I couldn't be sure. Later, I was sure. The point is that we didn't go to the Dairy Queen. We didn't go to Schrafft's or Schwab's.

We drove through a red light, snaking through the side roads until it seemed clear I had lost him. Or I thought I had: When I pulled up in front of the Savoy, I saw his car again.

It was parked across the street from my hotel.

34.

The Savoy is not a hotel. Look, I know I just called it that, Doc, but I didn't mean to, so strike that from the record and note only that we parked down the block from the Fairlane and waited to see what the driver would do.

The lights were coming on up and down Wilshire. The DeSoto dashboard glowed. Jo had nothing to do with her hands, until she reached for the silver crucifix that dangled between her breasts and felt it with her fingers like a rosary. I hadn't seen it before. Well, of course she was Catholic. So was I. Emphasis on *was*.

The engine ticked.

The man in the Fairlane hardly moved. His left arm dangled from the window, fingers flicking ash from a butt. But he didn't leave the car. In fact, he wasn't doing anything except listening to the radio. We heard the "Boom Boom" song.

"What do you suppose he's doing?" Jo asked.

"Waiting for me."

"Why?"

"He's followed me before."

"So?"

"So you can't save me, Jo. You might as well tell me what Jeanne said."

I won't go into what it took to get the information. It was incomplete anyway. She hadn't even heard Jeanne's whole story, in part because I had interrupted it. But it involved the fact that, toward the end of her life, a paranoid Marilyn, believing she was bugged, would (Jeanne said) make and take certain calls only from pay phones, which she haunted around the clock. But very late at night, in bed, washing pills down with champagne, she called her best friends—Jeanne among them. She had done this on her last night, when she sounded "strange," Jeanne had said.

"She was scared," Jo said. "She wanted Jeanne to come over."

"Why?"

"She wouldn't say. That's what Jeanne said. She didn't want 'them' to hear."

"Who was 'them'?"

"Whoever had tapped the phone. Whoever was listening through the walls. Whoever was wiretapping her, making the tape of her life. And death. Someone kept calling her—a woman—saying, 'You stay away from Bobby.' She was scared—no, terrified. So she begged her to come over. But Jeanne was tired. She said her own phone rang one last time that night, after she'd talked to Marilyn. Well, it must have been Marilyn, she said. It just kept ringing. For minutes, it rang. Until it stopped, that small ting lingering in the house long after she'd hung up. Jeanne took the phone off the receiver, took another pill or two, and fell asleep."

It was dark. I looked out the window. The man wasn't leaving.

I opened the car door.

"What are you doing?"

"Going up there," I said.

"What if he follows you?"

"Honk the horn three times and call the cops."

I stepped onto Wilshire.

"Ben."

I crossed the street and went into the lobby. It was empty, the bar closed, the elevator out of order.

It was always out of order.

So I took the stairs.

35.

I heard the radio from the bedroom when I opened the door. Someone had opened the cupboards in the kitchen. Someone had opened the refrigerator and taken out the milk. The bottle sat on the low piece of wall that separated the dining area from the kitchenette. A cloudy empty glass sat on the table.

I went into the bedroom.

"You're late," Rose said.

She was sitting on my bed. She wore a new dress: a gray Norman Norell that was as neatly pressed and folded as a restaurant napkin. She wore a simple strand of pearls. She had dyed her hair a simmering blond and wore a slick of bold red lipstick. A postcard-sized patent leather clutch sat on her lap.

Max played with Monopoly pieces on the floor.

"What are you doing here?" I said.

"You have custody tonight. How many times do I have to tell you?"

"I don't want custody."

Max looked up.

"Jesus, Ben, that's rich." She stood. "First you fight me, then say you don't want him. How's he supposed to take that?"

"It's not safe here. For Max."

"That's what I've been saying all along: this place. How can you live like this?"

"Please, Rose. Take him."

"I can't," she said. "I'm late."

"For what?"

"A date."

"The guy in the Fairlane?"

"None of your business."

"You hire him to follow me?"

"None of your business."

"Rose?"

I took Max to the movies. It was a new type of movie that used three projectors showing three versions of the same film on a curved screen. Did you see *This Is Cinerama*? I didn't, either. Rose saw it with Max and for weeks afterward all she could talk about was that damn roller coaster. It impressed Maxwell, too, which is why he wanted to see *The Wonderful World of the Brothers Grimm* at the Warner.

I was running out of cash, but I bought balcony seats for $1.45 each. The whole thing gave me a headache, which wasn't helped by the fact that I couldn't stop wondering about everyone else in the theater. There was, for instance, the solitary man who sat behind us. The theater was almost empty. Why did he sit behind us?

"Come on, Max," I whispered. "Let's move."

"Why, Dad?"

"I don't like these seats."

So we got up and moved.

Max loved the movie, which was the whole point. He kept talking about the movie's train ride as I drove back to the Savoy. He was talking about the ride when I began barricading the apartment door. I put a chair up under the doorknob, then moved the couch against the door.

"What are we doing, Dad?"

"Building a fort."

I tucked him in, the thimble in his fist.

"Mind if I ask you a question, sport?"

"You just did."

"Who's your mom's friend?"

"Uncle Daddy."

"Daddy? Really?"

Max nodded.

"You like him?"

"Okay."

"He's nice to you?"

"Sure."

"What's he do?"

"Makes books."

"He's a writer?"

"I don't know. They're about horses."

"What kind of horses?"

He didn't answer.

He was already asleep.

I went to get the Wild Turkey.

Morning flipped on like the jump-cut beginning of a movie after minutes if not hours of a black screen. There were no dreams behind it. I couldn't remember any, sitting up with the light through the window. It was too bright, the sun too high.

It was 2:15.

"Hey," I said. "Max."

I stood, still in my clothes. The barricade was undisturbed. I walked to the dining area just off the kitchen. I saw a half-empty bowl of Trix on the table. The spoon hung from the edge. His thimble sat in the milk that spattered the tablecloth.

"Max?"

I walked down the hall, touching the walls, then stopped with my hands on the frame of the door looking into my bedroom, the room where he slept.

The bed was unmade, but Max wasn't in it.

"Max?"

I thought of it then. I hadn't before.

I turned to the bathroom.

"Max."

The Sony is a standard reel-to-reel, and for a long time it records nothing. It just turns. We have already gone through ten tapes. You tap the last cigarette in the ashtray; the smoke rises in a long line to the bulb. It breaks apart in the paddles of the ceiling fan.

Your pack of Chesterfields sits on the table.

"What happened to your son?" you ask.

"You tell me."

"You're under arrest."

"I shouldn't have done what I did," I said. "I shouldn't have gone to Ciro's. I should have taken up knitting instead."

"What happened to your son?"

I say nothing.

You stand, pushing the chair away, and walk to the door, where you call for the guard.

Again there is a hollow booming, the jangling of keys, the dark shape opening the door. You turn once to look at me. “Think about it,” you say as you step into the hall.

And you are gone again.

The headline on the paper you have left behind is large and black:

U.S. GETS READY TO ATTACK

At some point I fall asleep on the floor.

I dream through the pain as the pills wear off, the image of the woman on all fours behind my eyes: crawling around, James straddling her and lifting her up, blasted out of her mind, Sinatra saying, “These are pretty sick, aren’t they?”

Yes they are: really sick.

The wait is worse this time. Maybe two or three days. The hunger for the bitter pills is growing; so is the pain—until “Okay,” I say in (what?) my third day? I can’t tell. “Okay,” I say. “You’ve won.”

No sound.

I turn the Sony on and press RECORD.

THURSDAY, AUGUST 16

36.

He was lying on the bathroom tiles, looking like a crumpled heap of laundry in his rumpled T-shirt and accordioned corduroys, his head turned toward the cabinet under the sink, arms raised against the floor, as if saying, "Don't shoot!" The brown hair was damp and curled against his neck. His shirt was hiked up in the back, so that I could see his precious skin.

I've never felt such a rush of dread. Everything went red. Outside sounds disappeared, replaced by my heart pumping, blood through ventricles and veins, which was all I heard as I picked up my son.

He was blue.

"Max!"

I don't remember what happened. I can piece it all together in retrospect, knowing the numbers I must have called, the people I'd spoken to and seen, the lights in the room and against the windows of the ambulance outside.

All of this is a matter of record. But the memory itself has gone, so entirely that I wish that someone would tell me exactly what happened on the morning when I sat, holding the thimble, in the waiting room. I lit a cigarette, though there was no ashtray, and the woman who sat behind the desk rose like an angry nurse, because she *was* an angry nurse, and told me to put it out.

Tomorrow would be Day One.

I walked outside, standing under the awning staring into the lot and the highway past the trees that edged the lawn. There was the sound of traffic. I finished the cigarette and flicked it into the bushes.

The taxi pulled in, Rose lurching with her pocketbook onto the sidewalk.

"Rose." I stepped toward her.

Her eyes were blind with fury. "You go to hell!" she screamed.

I took the thimble from my pocket and held it out to her.

She closed it in her fist and turned away.

I followed her through the doors that led to the room where the people were waiting on stretchers. She knew where she was going. She was *allowed* to go. But I was brought back to the emergency room by the nurse who said, as she had said before, that I was not allowed.

"I'm his father," I said.

"The doctor is still questioning."

I see the tape turning on the table now. I look up and see the metal door, still locked. I turn back to the tape and shout into the microphone: "Are you listening? You asked what happened, and I'm trying to tell you: He was poisoned, for Christ's sake. Are you listening?"

I'm not sure how much time passes. It seems like hours. It is possibly, probably, more like minutes. I am waiting for you, of course, Doctor; at some point, I hear the clanking down the hall, the jangling of keys.

The metal door opens, and you step inside.

You sit, as always, across from me and nod. It looks as if you have washed your hair, even if you haven't.

"I see that you're recording already," you say. "Very diligent of you."

"I'm a diligent guy."

"I appreciate that."

From your pocket you withdraw a vial of Novrils.

I reach—

"Tell me what happened to Max first."

"They were in the cereal."

"What?"

"The Toy Surprise was supposed to be a purple dinosaur. That's what it said on the box. But the *real* Surprise was gone. And in its place—"

You don't believe me, but I am telling the truth—and the truth is that, after I carried Max, like a rag doll, to the couch, and made certain he was breathing, and after I rushed to call the ambulance from the lobby, I ran back to the apartment and saw the Trix spilled on the floor in the dining room, the milk in the bowl streaked with all those unnatural colors.

And mostly the color was yellow.

37.

I waited all afternoon in the emergency room, where I didn't think of Marilyn Monroe. I was doing what Curphey had told me to do. I didn't think of Marilyn when I paced between the packed rows of plastic seats and didn't think of Marilyn when I heard, at three, that Max was finally awake. I didn't think of Marilyn when the cops arrived and asked if I was Ben Fitzgerald.

"Yes," I said, and didn't think about Marilyn when they asked the same questions that you are asking now, Doc, on this, the tenth tape. It's not easy to explain, and with four Novrils in my blood I can't tell how far away the floors have fallen anyway.

"What happened to your son?" they asked.

I couldn't tell the cops the truth. It would have seemed crazy. So I simply said that Max had gotten into the medicine cabinet and, thinking they were "candy," had eaten a few yellow jackets.

"Why would you leave narcotics within reach of the boy?"

"They weren't in reach. They were in the medicine cabinet. In a yellow vial."

The yellow vial that is sitting on the table before us now, Doc: Item No. 2.

They let me see Max around six. I went in through the double doors and saw him behind the curtains, tubes in his nose, a hep-lock drip taped to his arm. I saw a speck of blood on the bandage.

Rose stood by the resident on the other side of the gurney, holding Max's hand. She turned when she saw me. "What are you doing?"

The resident said, "It's okay, ma'am. The doctor said—"

"I don't care what the doctor said. For crissakes, don't you see the burns?"

"Rose."

"There's a fucking pattern here."

"Rose, be quiet," I said.

"Don't you fucking tell me to be quiet! You almost killed him!"

"He's crying, Rose," I said.

"Then why don't you leave? You want to help your son, Ben? Leave."

She was right, I supposed. They wanted me to disappear, so I disappeared. I got home around seven. There were messages at the bar from Jo. I didn't call her back.

I was on vacation.

I called the Pick-Carter in Cleveland from the lobby and said, "I'm checking on a reservation for a Benjamin Fitzgerald."

"Checking. Yes, sir. Here it is. He hasn't yet arrived."

"That's okay. I wonder if you could do me a favor."

"Anything."

"I need you to send a few postcards."

I didn't think about Marilyn when I lit another cigarette or when I smoked another three, or five, the temperature at ninety-four. I didn't think—tried not to think—of Marilyn when I learned, at the newsstand, that the Suicide Squad had released their findings at a press conference:

Marilyn Monroe, described as a moody woman with a death wish, died a probable suicide of a lethal combination of sleeping tablets and knockout pills taken in "one or two gulps," the Coroner's office revealed yesterday.

A final toxicological report showed the 36-year-old beauty died from sleeping pills and chloral hydrate. Either dose would have resulted in her death, according to Coroner Theodore J. Curphey.

"Miss Monroe had suffered from psychiatric disturbances for a long time. She experienced severe fears and frequent depressions. Mood changes were abrupt and unpredictable."

Curphey explained that death occurred from four to eight hours before her body was found at 3:30 a.m. on Aug. 5—

"Bullshit," I said, and turned to the *Mirror* in search of Jo's column, "The Voice of Hollywood." Instead of the truth I found the usual: "'I love Bob Hope!' says Screen Siren Jeanne Carmen, who happens to be a whiz of a trick-shot golfer. 'Whatta guy!' Seems the charming Miss Carmen, with whom we recently shared cocktails at the ever-reliable Ciro's, has been making the studio rounds to reignite her career—on and off the links."

I read the whole column, then read it again: There was nothing in it about Marilyn, the Kennedys, or the mysterious phone calls.

I went back to the lobby and dialed Jo's number—dialed, that is, every number but one, hanging there with the cord in my hand, finger poised on that last digit, 5, and thought of Max.

I hung up.

I spent the next couple of days on vacation, which meant that I went to the hospital when Rose was not there, trying to erase whatever ideas she had put in my son's head. But on the third day, when I showed up, he was gone: "He's fine, Mr. Fitzgerald," the nurse said. "They released him yesterday."

I called Rose in El Segundo. Sweat soaked my T-shirt: worse than the night sweats Marilyn suffered from, I thought, though I didn't think of Marilyn at all.

"The number you have reached," the operator said, "has been disconnected. The number you have reached . . ."

MONDAY, AUGUST 20

38.

The sign outside my former house read FOR RENT. There was a number to call, along with the name of the real-estate company. I parked across the street, wiped the hair over my forehead, trying to look presentable, and walked in the rain to the front door. I rang the doorbell as a plane roared overhead, coming in for a landing.

I rang the bell again, thinking that they hadn't heard on account of the plane; no one answered. I knocked, then pounded, and finally tried my key.

She had changed the locks.

The screen door banged shut as I walked through the mud around back. The grass seed I had planted had washed away, leaving patches of muck. Wooden sticks with hopeful plastic pictures of vegetables poked up from the empty garden Rose had planted along one side of the house.

In the back, a wet sandbox and rusted swings and all my stuff: soaked books, the old model train I had bought for Max's last birthday and assembled in the basement, my typewriter, a stack of jazz albums Rose had never liked, a few 8mm W. C. Fields movies, and a baseball bat.

I didn't know what to do. The rain was steady but relentless from a sky that did not change. I returned to the front of the house, squeezing along the bushes below the wet front window. I cupped my hands around my eyes and stared into the living room.

The furniture was gone.

Now, at 5678, you want to know what I did next. That's exactly what you say:

"What did you do next?"

"The phone was disconnected," I say. "I didn't know where my wife was. She didn't work; I couldn't find her in an office. So I did the only thing that I could think of."

"Which was?"

I parked across the street from El Segundo Elementary. The clock on the dashboard wasn't right—it seemed no clock ever was—but I was early, so all I had to do was watch and wait. The wind wings went back and forth, clearing my vision of the street ahead, but I couldn't see the school through the driver's-side window.

So I rolled it down.

The school's double doors opened into the rain that fell with a hiss and the summer school students rushed out with colored umbrellas and rubber galoshes. I heard the shouts and laughter as they tottered across the quad to the long line of buses and cars.

I waited for Max.

He seemed to be the last kid, walking hand in hand with the teacher down the sidewalk.

My face was spattered with rain and I blinked against it as I shouted, "Max!"

The teacher looked up; Max, too, looked up and smiled and waved.

I waved back.

Max ran so happily that his feet got ahead of his body, giving an extra little kick in the middle of each stride; I thought he might overbalance himself and tumble straight into the street.

I opened the car door, determined to catch him before he ran through the crosswalk where the man in the raincoat held the STOP sign and a whistle.

But Max wasn't running to me.

He didn't even see me.

He ran to the vehicle parked two spots ahead.

It was the Ford Fairlane.

Take a picture of this. They did, after all. The wings made rhythmic sounds against the glass and the radio sparked as lightning hit, and I pulled from the space near the crosswalk between buses and almost hit the car.

That was when I saw the flash. It wasn't lightning.

It came through my back window. I turned and couldn't see anyone. I wondered who had taken it.

"See this?" From your stained evidence folder, I pull out another 8 × 10. In it, you can see my car pulling into the road along the school as I followed the Ford.

Another picture. And another. All trying to prove, I suppose, that I was harassing my wife and son in addition to allegedly killing the woman.

"Allegedly," you say. "You said *allegedly*."

"Yes."

"Look at the images. They're in front of you, Ben. You were following the car. You followed the car in the rain from El Segundo up 405 to the Wilshire exit. You followed it until the driver realized you were following him, and lost you."

"He was speeding."

You take a drag on the cigarette. "I want you to hear something." You press STOP, remove the two reels from the bulky Sony, and with the cigarette still burning, put the tapes into two separate cardboard boxes, which you mark with indelible black marker.

You find another tape, this one marked "Rose: evidence 9/17/62." You put it in the recorder and with your yellow forefinger press PLAY.

"—sure he was drinking." (Rose's voice.) "His father was a drunk. He was always taking Ben on trips to follow searchlights. They'd end up in used car lots. They'd end up in a bar. Ben was desperate to escape this—I've told you that. But it's bred in the bone. It lives in your blood. Some things don't change. Some things are inevitable. Doctor, I read a book once that said that in relationships you either put deposits in or take withdrawals out of an emotional bank account. Together you have this account. And if you take a withdrawal, it's hard to put the money back. You have to put back twice as much to get to the point where you were before, if that makes sense."

The doctor: "Sure."

"It was just so obvious. I mean, you've seen the photographs."

"Which?"

"The ones taken of him going into that Melrose bar. The ones that showed him . . . fucking that whore in the Malibu hotel."

"That came later."

"All those bottles of Canadian Club."

"That's all later."

"But that isn't even the point. Nothing he would ever put back could compensate for what happened to Max. The Nembutals. And burn marks."

"*What* burn marks?"

"He burned him. With his cigarettes."

"You said they were bug bites."

"They were cigarette burns."

"*You* smoke cigarettes, too."

"They were Kents. I could tell the difference."

"How?"

"I could *smell* it."

Now you press STOP and look at me again. You adjust your glasses against the bridge of your nose. Your skin looks damp and green, like something underwater. "How did you find out where they were living?"

"I called the realtor. The number on the sign outside our house."

But first I called Jo.

"What the hell happened?" she said. "Where the hell have you been?"

"Didn't you get my postcard?"

"I got your postcard. What were you doing in Cleveland?"

"I'll explain later," I said. "Right now I need your help."

39.

Remember," I said as I parked across the street, smiling through my clenched jaw. "We're the Carnahans. You're Evelyn. I'm Paul."

"I remember," Jo said.

"You're pregnant, and we need a house to raise the child, and we don't have the money, so it needs to be a starter house—here," I said, "in El Segundo."

"Got it."

I'd told Jo to dress down as much as she could, since I did not want the real-estate agent to know that she was, in fact, the sort of woman who lunched at Romanoff's and dined and drank silver draughts of gin at Ciro's. But Jo, being Jo, dressed in a sort of Cecil Beaton version of poverty: flat formal surfaces and lush piled fabric in a wide variety of . . . That's what she said anyway. To me, she looked like Grace Kelly in *The Grapes of Wrath.*

She looked out the window at the house with its bald lawn and the sad FOR RENT sign.

The realtor, a nervous-looking woman in a blue shift, paced the driveway, holding an umbrella like a riding crop.

The rain had stopped.

"This is where you lived?" Jo asked.

"Sure."

"Jesus, how creepy."

"No editorializing. Come on."

I got out of the car, opened the shotgun side for Jo, her hand sliding into the crook of my arm as we walked to the driveway.

The realtor turned, the nervous look replaced by the mask of a smile. "Why, hello!" she said with a faint British accent. "You must be the Carnahans."

"The very," I said.

She gave Jo the up and down, eyes lingering. "Well then," she said. "Come with me."

"What's all this junk?" Jo asked, pointing to my old belongings along the side of the house.

"Don't worry," the realtor said. "They're having it all removed. It's what didn't sell."

"Sell?"

"In the garage sale."

I looked at Jo. She sniffed.

The tour of the house wasn't the point. I knew the house. Still, it was interesting to see what Rose had thrown out and packed up, what she had deemed worth saving and what she had left behind as junk. And for the sake of the illusion, we let the agent go through the motions, telling us that the house was "modern" (meaning prefab) and had "good bones" (meaning it needed renovations). Jo asked a few innocuous questions, but it wasn't until the end that I got the information I needed, the information I had come for.

"I'm a little concerned about the noise from the airport," Jo said. "All those planes."

"Oh, that's what we call ocean noise," the realtor said.

"It's *not* ocean noise. It's *airplane* noise."

"But you'll get used to it. People get used to anything."

"I'm not 'people,' " Jo said.

I nudged her.

"Did you know you can drive out to Imperial and watch the takeoffs?" the realtor said. "There's a lookout station near the airport."

"Like a scenic overlook?"

"You could say that. The rent is quite inexpensive. And it's an up-and-coming location, certainly. Confidentially, between the three of us, I think the previous owners had . . . problems."

"What kind of problems?" Jo asked.

"Well, there was a separation. And a child. It was all very painful. Apparently, between the three of us and the lamppost, the father was abusing his son."

Jo gasped. "Really. What kind of man would—?"

"What kind of man indeed," the realtor said. "The good news is this very nice young woman has found a new friend."

"A friend?"

"A protector of sorts. Oh, it's too soon to say it's any kind of relationship, if you know what I'm saying, but the man has taken pity on her. That's what she told me. She's living in his apartment. She feels 'safe' there."

"How nice," Jo said. "Now, what did you say his name was?"

TUESDAY, AUGUST 21

40.

I found the address for the man named "John Rawlston" in the phone book: Verona Gardens. The place had once been a tony nightclub—it was now a hotel—on Hollywood Boulevard. Rudy Villarosa and his Cuban Dream Orchestra had for twenty years broadcast a show from the upstairs Club Room every Saturday at 10 P.M. In his introduction, Mr. Villarosa always said, with a fake Spanish accent (his real name had been Fred Floyd), "Welcome to the Verona Gardens on Hollywood Boulevard just east of Vine in the City of Film: Hollywood, California."

They played "The Hummingbird." They played "Brother, Can You Spare a Dime?" They played "Deep Night." But before long the red damask booths began to fray. The cigarette burns on tabletops multiplied like measles. The radio show was canceled. The film stars with their diamond earrings and bow ties moved to Sunset, Ciro's, Mocambo, and the Garden of Allah—and in their place emerged a desperate people just one step away from foreclosure.

"Mr. Rawlston, please," I said to the man behind the front desk.

"Who?"

"I'm looking for Johnny Rawlston."

"He isn't in right now. May I take a message?"

"Tell him Ben Fitzgerald is looking for him. I'll be in the bar."

Look, I knew Verona Gardens, Doc. You know that. The piss-elegant saloon was no longer elegant but still smelled of piss. Cigarette burns dotted the balding carpet like bullet holes. Burning ashes lit your dreams. Someone was always unscrewing the lightbulbs. Someone else was stealing your happiness, if not your car.

I don't remember how much time passed, but there were four Tom Collins glasses sitting on the table with limes in the bottom when I stepped into the phone booth and called Jo.

"I've been trying to reach you," she said. "Where are you?"

"Verona Gardens."

"What?"

"To meet Johnny Rawlston."

"You mean Johnny Roselli."

"The name's *Rawlston*."

"I did some checking. His real name is Roselli. R-O-S-E-L-L-I."

"This should mean something to me?"

"Are you sitting down?"

"I'm in a phone booth."

"You should be sitting down."

"I can't sit in a phone booth."

"You heard of *He Walked by Night*?"

"Should I?"

"It's a movie. Johnny 'produced' it."

"So he's a producer. So I'm still standing."

"It was a ruse. Johnny was pulling strings to make himself respectable after he got out of jail."

"Why?"

"God, I love how you keep delivering the straight lines."

"So give me the punch line, George Jessel."

"Johnny Roselli is also known as—let's see here; I wrote this down—'Filippo Sacco, Handsome Johnny, James Roselli.' He's, um, the Chicago outfit's man in L.A. He was part of the Capone Syndicate. Convicted of federal labor racketeering charges for masterminding the Mob shakedown of the Hollywood unions. Sprung in 1947. Now he calls himself a PR guy and a consultant, but his fingers are still in any number of pies. He takes bets at Santa Anita."

"Horse books," I said.

"What?"

"My son calls him Uncle Daddy. Says he makes 'horse books.' "

"Well, he sure as hell didn't write *My Friend Flicka*."

"Okay, I'm sitting down now."

"Hang on," she said, and told me a story:

Johnny Stompanato had been Lana Turner's lover (she said). They wrote letters to each other. *Extreme* letters. Lana's were addressed to "Daddy Darling" and "Dearest Precious Heart." The Sweater Girl wrote of "our love, our hopes, our dreams, our sex and longings." She wrote, "You're my man." She penned these letters even during periods when, she later testified, she was being beaten by the same Precious Heart who was fucking her, the Daddy Darling her daughter, Cheryl, eventually shot.

You can see pictures of him dead on the floor.

"I don't see what that has to do with—"

"Say you're handsome, Ben. And charming."

"That's a stretch."

"Say you send a girl flowers every day. You lay on the veneer. Chocolates. The fine car. The mink. The dinners and the Dom. All of which a man uses to disguise the fact that he wants to bed a woman. All of which allows the woman to pretend that whatever carnal interest she may have in the man is something else when, you know, what she *really* wants is to be thrown on the bed, in the back of the car, in a bathroom stall, and ravished."

"Where are you going with this?"

"It didn't happen overnight," she said. "It happened over the course of months. But at one point, as Lana put it, 'I had fallen for him,' and whatever he needed to know or to gain he got from her through sex. And so."

"So what?"

"Johnny Stompanato was doing to Lana what Johnny Roselli is doing to your wife: extorting her. Sexually. He wanted information: Your Social Security number. Your bank account. Your license number. And then—"

"Then what?"

"Just do me a favor, Ben."

"Sure."

"Get out of Verona Gardens."

There was a pounding at the door.

"Ben?"

The Tall Man from Ciro's was standing outside.

And he was smiling.

41.

The archetypal American story is arguably the story of the Guy Who Does Not Give Up. You can achieve anything if you just Put Your Mind to It. Horatio Alger. The Little Engine That Could. Hey, the Mafia, too. But Ragged Dick never had to deal with Bobby Kennedy. And the Little Engine wasn't stopped on his way up the hill by LAPD goons or some guy named John Rawlston or Roselli who had something to do with both the Santa Anita racetrack and my wife.

I was done. I wanted to quit. But here's Johnny:

"You must be Ben," he said.

"Oh, actually."

"Front desk says you're Ben. Well, you must be. Fitzgerald, right?"

"Right."

"Call me Johnny."

He reached into his jacket, removed a business card, and handed it to me. It said "consultant." He then removed a pack of cigarettes, revealing a flash of what looked like a gun. He put a cigarette into his mouth and handed the pack to me.

"I don't smoke."

"Not what I heard." He flipped his lighter, lit the cigarette.

"What did you hear?"

"I hear you smoke a lot even though your son has asthma 'n' that you don't have money 'n' that you keep your kid in a bad hotel."

"It's not a hotel."

"Was the last time I looked, Don."

"Name's Ben."

"You know, I love that part in *Naked City* when you go to find the boxer and he's doing sit-ups. What'd they use in that? Chloroform?"

"Who told you about that?"

"I saw *Naked City*."

"Jeanne Carmen?"

"Nice girl."

"You know Jeanne Carmen."

"I know a lot of people. I'm a *producer*."

"So I've heard."

"You've seen my movies?"

"Never saw *He Walked by Night*."

"How about *The Empty Glass*?"

"Can't say that I have."

"You'd like it, Don. All about the death of an actress. So they find her dead on the bed but the glass was empty. Now, let me ask you something," he said. "How did she swallow those pills?"

The place was like one of those department-store showrooms where the spines of coverless books are turned to the back of the shelves, so as not to screw up the color scheme. The style was strictly Mid-Century Motel Room. The picture above the couch against the left wall showed a spiky torero in some Spanish bullring. On the other side of the couch stood a tall cage in which a bright green and orange parrot hung on a mini-trapeze. His plumed head bobbed up and down.

My wife's nightgown lay on the bed above her slippers.

My son's Monopoly board sat on the floor, *real* bills standing in for play money.

Johnny took his jacket off and laid it on the sheet. He untied his shoelaces, took a flask from his vest pocket, and handed it to me.

"No thanks."

"Have a seat." He patted the spot beside him.

I took my hat off and sat. "You were saying."

"Saying what?"

"How did she swallow those pills?"

He took a deep swig from the flask and squinted, eyes watering. "I asked *you* that question," he said. "Say, I wish I knew. The whole thing is like a movie. I know the beginning. I'm puzzling over the middle. But the end is what's *really* bothering me. You know what I think the problem is?"

"What?"

"Lack of historical accuracy. Bad source material. I need to do more research. I need to know about the last weekend Marilyn spent alive. It was at Cal-Neva Lodge out on the border between Nevada and California. Sinatra was there," he said. "And something happened in Chalet fifty-two, where Marilyn was staying. Something bad."

"What?"

"That's what I need to know."

"What makes you think I can help?"

"I'm a patriot, Ben. I enlisted at thirty-seven. They didn't want me. I was 'physically unfit.' That's what they said. I had neuritis and arthritis in my spine. I had tuberculosis. But I kept going down to the board out in Westwood until I was inducted. Landed in Normandy and went through the Rhineland into Central Europe. That's where I learned German," he said, "from the whores."

"How?"

"They called them Sleeping Dictionaries. You get them in bed and they whisper in your ear and that is how I learned the language."

"I don't follow."

"It wasn't hard to reach your wife. She put ads in the paper. She was dating some old fanook named Mr. Charles. *Reginald* Charles. It wasn't hard to take the fat fuck out into the back and slit his belly just a little. It wasn't hard to be a comfort when I found out that her ex had either poisoned her son or left drugs out so her son could think they were candy. So I start to see your wife. And so she softens up. It's not long before she tells me something."

"What?"

"You found a diary."

"I don't know what you're talking about."

"I told you I'm a patriot. We got the vote in West Virginia. You think Kennedy would have stood a chance otherwise? Humphrey had the state sewn up until we went out with piles of cash and baseball bats. You know what they think about Micks out there? The bleeding ugly Irish?"

"No."

"Why are Christmas lights and Irishmen alike?"

"Half of them are broke and the other half don't work," I said.

"So we changed all that—and the first thing Bobby does after big brother gets elected is go after Jimmy Hoffa. You read *The Enemy Within*. Still, it didn't end there. You know the Brown Derby?"

"Sure."

"That's where first I met Robert Maheu."

He was a barrel of a man who slipped (Johnny said) into the round booth in the Derby's back room. He worked for Howard Hughes and was a fixer for the CIA, having once made a porn film that showed a Sukarno look-alike having sex with a woman in Moscow. He told Johnny that the government was preparing to invade Cuba. Castro had overthrown Batista in 1958, kicking the Mob's casinos out of Havana. The West celebrated the coup at first—but it wasn't long before Castro's Communism became clear, and (worse) a missile base now existed ninety miles off the coast of Florida.

It was February 1961.

"What if," Maheu asked Johnny in the Derby that day, "you'd had the opportunity to get rid of Hitler in 1932?"

"I would have blown him away."

"Anyone with a soul would have, sure. And you have it, John. That's why we want to work with you."

"Who's 'we'?"

"The CIA. Help us eliminate the Beard."

"Now, how's that gonna work?" Johnny asked. "Feds follow me everywhere. They go to my shirtmaker to see if I'm paying cash, for crissake."

"You won't have trouble. We'll pay you a hundred and fifty thousand—in bills. But if you say Bob Maheu brought you into this, I will deny and deny. Swear I don't know what you're talking about."

Now Johnny took another swig from the flask and handed it to me.

"No thanks."

"Suit yourself." He swigged again. "You know what botulinum is?"

"No."

"Now, that's a nerve toxin. It binds to nerve cells, which stops them from releasing a neurotransmitter—fancy name for what makes nerves work. If a neurotransmitter stops functioning, you get paralysis—tongue, ribs. Guinea pigs don't die from it—who knew? But guess what?"

"What?"

"Monkeys do. I watched them. The CIA made a pill, see. They were gonna get rid of Castro with botulinum first and *then* move in. We had a man with the pill in a restaurant. He was going to drop it in Castro's soup, but the Kennedys pulled the plug. So they sent all our boys into an ambush."

You know the drill, Doc: On April fifteenth, U.S. bombers disguised as Cuban revolutionary planes flew over Cuba. On Bahía de Cochinos, American-trained Cuban exiles filled the beaches, but the rebels had been tipped off by the whores in the hills. The boats landed and blood flowed. No air cover. No backup—thanks to the Kennedys. The soldiers were slaughtered like (I can't help it, Doc) pigs.

"So we got JFK elected. So we offered to assassinate the enemy. Now I'm a patriot: I took no money. And what happened? After Cuba, my shirtmaker calls to say the Feds are hanging around again, asking if I paid cash. I was *still* paying cash. Except not the hundred and fifty thousand—money that I never took."

The phone rang.

Johnny picked up. "Hello." He frowned at me. "For you." He handed me the phone.

"Hi."

"Front desk," the man said. "A . . . Mr. Roselli here to see you."

"Who?"

"Johnny. Says you're expecting him."

"Look, this isn't my room—"

"He asked for *you*. Said you were there."

A white moth batted against the bulb stuck in the peeling ceiling, a charred halo surrounding the porcelain base. For a moment—it felt like hours—I heard that sound; then all sound dropped out.

I hung up.

"What was that?" Johnny said.

"Wrong number."

"Why would they call you?"

"I said it was a wrong number."

"Who knows you're here?"

"No one."

"I don't think that's true. Someone else wants that diary."

"I don't have it."

"No," he said. "But your girlfriend does."

A knock at the door. "Ben!" A voice: "It's Johnny."

"Jesus." He took the gun from his holster and walked to the door.

The curtains were blowing over the fire escape.

I stepped onto the metal and held the rickety rusted bars seven flights down to the ground; just across the street, Jo sat behind the wheel of a squad car.

42.

"What are you doing?" I asked, climbing into the side.

"Rescuing you," Jo said.

"This isn't your car."

"It's my friend's."

"It's a *cop* car."

"I have friends in high places," she said as she drove south, looking up. "Did you hear that?"

"Don't change the subject."

"You know how they always say that gunshots sound like fireworks?"

I nodded.

"That wasn't fireworks," she said.

43.

I hear the sirens all night. It's clear that things aren't going well. The papers are filled with doomsday news. Stocks are falling, grocery stores emptied out. People are making "lead" hats out of foil and covering their windows with duct tape. Schools have issued defense pamphlets in case of "enemy attack." It's everything but the moon filled with blood and the woman with WISDOM tattooed on her forehead. You can see things in the clouds, too, like the end of the world.

That's what happened in Cuba: One scenario, at least, in the sad series of scenarios that began with Ian Fleming. You know how they say that life imitates art? The truth is that life imitates spy stories.

One night at a fancy Georgetown dinner party in the spring of 1960, the baked Alaska had just been served when Senator John F. Kennedy, the host, leaned back and looked at his guest of honor, the James Bond author, with a cigar in his mouth. "If you had to eliminate Castro," Kennedy asked, "how would you do it?"

Well, Fleming thought this was a wonderful joke, a sort of party game and, half under the influence of some fine wine or another, he gave his James Bond answers:

Set off an elaborate fireworks display to terrify the Cubans into thinking the Second Coming was at hand.

Give Castro an exploding cigar.

Put an explosive into a Caribbean mollusk near where Castro scuba dives.

Or slip him a pill.

And now Jo was asking, "Ben, what happened back there?" I told her everything. Then I looked up to see that she was pulling into the Ambassador lot.

"Where are you going?"

"My apartment."

"Why?"

"Jesus, all these questions. Why is the sky blue? Why did Fido have to die? Do you know the way to San Jose?"

"Take 1-5 North."

"Now, let me ask *you* something," she said. "Did you leave your hotel light on?"

"It's not a hotel."

"The light was on in your room just now. I saw it from the car."

I'd never been inside the Ambassador—not even for a drink at the Grove. Well, I didn't have the money. Miss Monroe had begun her career here at a poolside modeling agency, and my friend Ed had once stayed in one of the Catalina bungalows. But now here I stood, hat in hand, in the lobby where the porters whisked valises on steel rollers to the banks of elevators filled with women in ermine and white dresses and long stockings, and the next thing I knew I was rising with Jo to her room overlooking the fake beach and the pool they called the Crystal Plunge on the third floor of the southern wing.

"Here." She opened the door and we stepped into a sitting area filled with faux Empire furniture and cream walls with stripes that Jo called *puce*, a fancy word for what happens when pink is left out in the sun for too long. An ivory Princess phone sat on a table under a mirror framed by a train of grasping cupids who had gotten tangled up in sheets but didn't seem troubled about it.

"Mabel, draw a bath, will you?" Jo called to an unseen maid, kicking her high heels off in the entryway and dropping her keys into a ceramic dish under the mirror.

"Yes, ma'am." The colored maid appeared, wearing a white apron around a black dress that whispered as she moved into the bathroom.

"Make yourself at home," Jo said. "Just promise to keep everything up to code."

"What code?"

"The Production Code. I'll sleep with my feet on the floor."

"You're inviting me to sleep over?"

"*Over* is the operative word," she said. "Not *with*. So promise: No excessive or lustful kissing, lustful embraces, suggestive postures or gestures, or any scenes that stimulate the lower or baser element."

"I promise."

"Complete nudity is not permitted. Including nudity in silhouette."

"I'll keep my pants on."

"No dancing that emphasizes indecent movements."

"I don't dance."

"Good."

Jo pulled her earrings off, one by one, making that little cupping gesture with the tilting head that was only one of the mysterious movements that women had collectively mastered.

She dropped her earrings in the bowl, then checked her watch. "Jesus, look at the time. I have to hurry."

"You're going—?"

"Out."

"With?"

"These questions! Delilah. She's my best friend. Oh, I know it's annoying, but she's having such trouble, and what kind of a friend would I be if I let her sob alone in her Miller all night?"

"She drinks Miller?"

"It's the Champagne of Beers."

"Yeah, but Champagne is the Champagne of Champagne."

"Well, she's a dirty boozy girl." She smiled. "Like me. Unzip me? There's a doll."

"Undressing scenes should be avoided," I said as the zipper whispered delicately through silk.

"Ah, but here's where we try to get around the censors!" she said as her dress crumbled to the floor.

"Miss Carnahan?" The maid stood at the bathroom door. "Your bath is ready."

The maid took me into what she called the "boo-door," as if it were a room for ghosts. It was a fancy name for "bedroom." There were fancy names for everything here. At the far end, a window overlooked the lawn. The window had puce lace curtains that dragged like bridal trains on the checkerboard floor. The mirrored dresser was opposite the bed.

"Make yourself at home," she said.

So I did.

I started opening the drawers. I went through the panties and bras and silk negligees in her dresser. I went through the bedside drawer and the hat boxes on the shelf above the closet.

I finally found the diary pages under the bed.

44.

You had to put the pieces together. I've said this already, Doc. Miss Monroe's writing wasn't always legible. But it seemed clear, as I've noted, that Sinatra was performing in the Celebrity Showroom at Cal-Neva Lodge on the weekend of July 28 and 29. He'd invited Marilyn to come, she wrote, "just for kicks."

But it was more than that. They called Cal-Neva "Heaven in the High Sierras," but that weekend it was pure hell. There were a lot of pills, and at some point Marilyn woke in her room with "James," she wrote. "I was naked but I never wanted this. I kept calling out for Frank but it wasn't till morning that I saw him standing there and he said if I said anything he'd bring Billy Woodfield the pictures and 'What pictures?' I asked. Well, the ones that he had taken.

"So I write this now to anyone who might find it and I had no choice. I couldn't say anything. They said, 'Leave the General alone' but I won't say 'the General' anymore I'm not protecting him anymore. His name is [redacted]."

After that, the only legible thing left was a fragment of Marilyn's final entry—written the day before she died:

August 4, 2:01 p.m.

All my hair things in the bag that I told you about, the one that I kept in the bathroom: They're gone. I couldn't find them. I told Pat about this, and she said not to worry.

"Don't get so upset," she said.

"Easy for you to say," I said. You who don't have to wake every morning at 5 for a call for a movie that—

What are you doing?" Jo asked. She was walking from the bathroom, hair done up in one of those elaborate towel turbans that only women know how to make. It looked like a pink hair dryer. Her silk bathrobe was white and monogrammed with her initials: JHC.

I held the pages up. "What were these doing under your bed?"

"Ben—"

"Did you take them from the bar?"

"I didn't want you to get hurt."

"I can take care of myself."

"Oh? Then how did you end up in a hotel room with Johnny Roselli?"

I read aloud from the pages: " 'The light was blue and yellow and the sun was high and everyone was gone and I could hardly raise my head everything too heavy including my fingers. The world was too much everything was too much and when I felt I could at least say a few words I called the operator. Billy Woodfield.' "

I looked up at Jo. "What does this mean?"

"What do you get when you cross an elephant—?"

"Who's Billy Woodfield?"

"Do I look like Nosferatu to you?"

"You mean Nostradamus."

"Whatever."

"Ma'am."

We both looked up.

It was the maid. "Miss Delilah on the phone, ma'am."

"One moment, Mabel. Hold here for a second?"

I watched her ass swing as she left the room.

I walked to the hall and tried to hear what she was saying. "No. It's . . . you what? Jesus, I'll be right over. My God, are you . . . ? Please. I'll . . . No. I'll . . . I can't talk now: He's here."

I ducked back into the room before she hung up. "Sorry, Ben," she said when she returned. "Delilah's waiting. At Pucini. And she's mad."

"Mad."

"She thinks I'm having an affair."

"Well, are you?"

"Not yet," she said.

45.

The only Billy Woodfield listed in the White Pages was a "Wm Read Woodfield" at "12336 Rye Scty." That was Studio City, off Ventura near the freeway. When I rang the bell, a big man answered wearing a wrinkled white shirt that was frayed around the collar. It ballooned around his belly like a sailcloth. He wore blocky black glasses. Gray hair feathered from both sides of his receding hairline.

"You the fella wants some pictures developed?" he asked.

"Yes."

"Say, that's a swell shirt." It was the shirt that Jo had given me, the one with the odd monogram. He fingered it with his right hand. "Where'd you get it?"

"Was a gift."

"Come in."

He led me inside his modest house. A golden retriever barked from its pen in the kitchen. We went down the hall to the office, which was also a darkroom. There was a solid desk behind which a clothesline of black-and-white 8 × 10s hung over a sink with a red light. Orange Kodak boxes were stacked on metal shelves. The room smelled of chemicals.

He gestured to the chair that sat across the desk from him. "Have a seat."

I did.

"Gotta confess that I haven't been doing much in the photo line lately." He sat behind the desk. "Been working on a book."

"Really? You're a writer?"

He nodded. "About Caryl Chessman. But you don't care about that." He lit a Viceroy, handing the pack to me. "Smoke?"

"I only smoke Kents," I said. "You have any Kents?"

"Viceroys."

"Tar kills you."

"Everything kills you."

"Tar kills you quicker. You should smoke Kents."

"I don't like Kents."

"So," I said. "Caryl Chessman."

"Sure."

"Was he innocent?"

"No. What a bastard. All kinds of people are so interested in his 'freedom.' Norman Mailer. Ray Bradbury. Billy Fucking Graham. What about the 'freedom' he gave those girls he stopped with his red light?"

"Sure," I said. "And Marilyn?"

"Who?"

"Marilyn Monroe."

"What about her?"

"You knew her."

His eyes narrowed. He adjusted his glasses. "Sure."

"Can you tell me about her?"

"Why?"

"I'm from the coroner's office." I showed him my credentials. "I need to know."

"Let me guess. The photo project you called me about? It doesn't exist."

"You guessed correctly."

"You don't need pictures developed."

"You are right, sir."

"Well, then we should do this properly. Like a drink?" he asked, pulling a half-empty (half-full) bottle of Crown Royal from the desk's bottom drawer.

"Sure."

"It's good stuff," he said. "Better than usual. I came into a bit of cash recently." He deposited the bottle on the desk, removed two dirty highball glasses from the same drawer, and laid them on his papers. And poured: a shot for me, a shot for him.

"Marilyn Monroe was a fabricator." He raised his glass. "Cheers. She lied. About everything. To herself, even. You know how they say that the goal of any real magician is to perform a trick that fools even himself?"

"No."

"Well, she was a real magician. She was always pulling imaginary rabbits out of hats. She was always writing, then rewriting, her life. Until even *she* didn't know what was true and what wasn't."

"So you're saying that whatever's in the diary is fake?"

"What diary?"

"The one that has your name in it."

I took the pages from my pocket and showed him the description of what had happened, or what might have happened, at the Cal-Neva Lodge.

His face went slack. He drained his glass of Crown Royal, filled it again to the top, and drank half of it, coughing. His eyes watered. "That's gibberish," he said.

"Is it? Why is your name here?"

"It's not my name."

"It's 'Billy Woodfield.'"

"Could be anyone's name."

"There's no other 'Billy Woodfield' in the Los Angeles phone book."

"Maybe he's unlisted."

"Bullshit. It says here Sinatra threatened to bring Billy Woodfield the pictures. What pictures?"

"Why should I tell you?"

"I'll go to the cops."

"They won't care, believe me."

"Because they're involved?"

"It's more than that. It's much more than that."

"How much more?"

He didn't answer.

"All right." I picked up the pages and stood from the desk. "Thanks for the drink."

I was all the way across his front lawn, reaching for the car door, when he called from the porch. "Buddy," he said. "Hey—"

Frank came by on Monday," he said back in the office. "I did work for him before, photographing his jet from one of the Conners helicopters out there in Santa Monica. So he had a roll of film that he wanted developed. Said it was 'high-level' stuff. Said there were people involved who you don't want to know were involved. And you don't want to know their names and shouldn't. Look, I'm not that kind of guy. I take pictures of movie stars. I write horror movies. I write *Death Valley Days*. You see 'The Unshakable Man'?"

"No."

"That was my episode. I don't want to get involved in any dirty business."

"But Frank gave you the film."

"Yeah."

"And gave you a lot of money to develop it."

"Sure."

"Hence the hooch."

"You got it."

"So what was on the film?"

He stood and walked past me to the door of his office, stepped out and looked around, then returned to the doorway, facing me, a shadow, his glass reflecting the light from above. "You know, Monroe annoyed me," he said. "Called at three A.M. like she called anyone she trusted. Woke my wife. Pissed her off. But it wasn't dirty business. She was just a friend. That's why it was hard to see her like that."

"Like what?"

"Like the way that she looked in these photos."

The photos were taken in Chalet 52 of the Cal-Neva Lodge, he said, looking through his files. A gooseneck lamp illuminated a stack of folders meticulously labeled in his neat hand. He looked at me from across the desk. I took notes on what he said.

The notes are right here, Doctor. They're part of the evidence in the box on your desk:

Item No. 3: A piece of notebook paper reading "Chalet 52" and "July 28."

Now you ask what these words mean.

Chalet 52:

Cal-Neva isn't visible from the road. It's set back in the woods. Three cabins have the best views of Crystal Bay and the Sierra

Nevadas. Bungalow 1 is reserved for Sinatra. The others are for "broads" and celebrity friends—Peter Lawford, Dean Martin. There are tunnels leading under these bungalows to the bar and the casino—a plus for Frank and his cronies. There is a trapdoor in the closet of Chalet 52, where Marilyn stayed on the night of July 28.

It was Sinatra's idea to take her there for the weekend, Billy said: She'd been lying low ever since singing her breathless "Happy Birthday" to the president. She threw the first ball at the new Dodger Stadium in Chavez Ravine on June 1—her last public appearance. But that was it. That was all. Sinatra said he wanted to celebrate the renewal of her contract with Fox. She had been fired from *Something's Got to Give* for being late. But she had powerful friends: Bobby Kennedy called Judge Rosenman, and Fox head Peter Levathes was told to reinstate and renegotiate the contract. So Sinatra flew her out on his private airplane, *Christina*: Plane N710E.

They landed in the Truckee Tahoe Airport.

July 28:

Dino performed that night in the Celebrity Showroom. He sang "That's Amore" and "Memories Are Made of This." He sang "Sway" and "Volare." But Monroe was not at Sinatra's table drinking her usual Dom Pérignon in her usual green Jean Louis dress and her usual high heels. She wasn't wearing the emerald earrings Sinatra had given her. She wasn't with her Mexican lover, José Bolaños.

She was locked in Chalet 52 high above the rocks over the bay, chasing the sleep that had always eluded her, curled up in the round bed with a bottle of Dom, hiding from the man she believed was still following her, the man she had seen peering through the windows.

She was sure (Billy said) she saw him walking past the window. She got up in the dark, took another Nembutal, and heard laughter through the woods. Music—Dino in his second set—coming from the lounge. Quarters clanking in the metal, tiny windows lighting up with cherries, cherries, cherries. Cocktail glasses clinking under big Nevada stars, laughter skimming over the black basin.

She opened the drapes, looked out the window and saw (she was certain) the imprint of a nose and lips on the glass. And there, too: writing.

One word on the window:

WHORE.

"Sinatra came by at three A.M., and she was upset," Billy said. "That's what he told me: 'Upset.' She had 'seen something outside,' she said, and was scared. She said, 'You don't believe me? Okay, look.' So she pointed to the window, and Frank walked to the window that looked down to the lake. He stood there for a long while."

"Did he see anything?" I asked.

"I didn't ask. You can't ask Frank anything. You only listen, so I listened as he told me that he went back to the round bed and told Marilyn nothing was there. She was panicked, though: She didn't believe him. 'You erased it,' she said. 'You wiped it off the window!' She went bonkers then."

"Why?"

"Because if he had erased the word WHORE from the dark glass, that meant it had been written from inside the room."

She panicked, looking under the bed and opening the closet. But the room was small and nothing was there. "The tunnels!" she shouted, running to the closet. "He came in through the trapdoor!"

Sinatra dragged at his cigarette, knowing what he had to do.

The vial of chloral hydrate sat, half-empty, on her bedside table. He had another bottle in his pocket. They were coming with more. "So," Billy said, "he told Marilyn to have another drink, and then there was a knock at the door. Sinatra said it was room service."

But it wasn't room service.

It was a man.

46.

Another drink?" Billy asked me.

"Sure."

He poured me another, then one for himself.

He drank his off in a gulp; I sipped tentatively at mine, but since he was already pouring himself another shot, I figured I should catch up. I swallowed it. "Who was the man?"

"Oh, you don't want to know. We should just stop talking now. We've already said too much."

"*You* have."

"That's what I mean. I want to show you something."

He reached into a drawer, removed a paperback with a red cover, opened it, and read aloud: "Didn't I have Borden's ironclad assurance a Big Story was out there somewhere in our sprawling, sports-starved metropolis just waiting for Charley Evans, columnist and feature writer, to break it? What more did I need, a Ouija board?"

He put the book down and smiled with pained resignation. "There's more," he said. "Korea, psychology, the dark side of boxing, but it's all pretty blah."

"What is it?"

"Caryl Chessman's novel. He wrote three books in prison. One of them this: *The Kid Was a Killer.* And it's not about his life. It's about boxing. Well, sure it would be fascinating to read a novel from a killer and kidnapper if the whole thing weren't so tedious."

"I don't know what this has to do with Cal-Neva."

"Caryl stopped women with a red light and raped them. The man in the photos drugged and raped a young star. Don't step into that black circle, Ben. I know there's a Big Story out there somewhere in our sprawling, blood-starved metropolis just waiting for Ben Fitzgerald, deputy coroner, to break it. But Big Stories are dangerous. Do yourself a favor: Walk away from this. Get back to your life."

"Who was the man with Sinatra at the lodge?"

"Christ, you really want to know."

I nodded.

His hands were shaking. He had a drink. And then another. And still another for good measure. Then he held the bottle out to me.

"No thanks."

"It's good stuff. I just bought it." He was slurring his words. "Came into a little cash just recently. I tell you that?"

"You told me that."

He removed a folder from his desk and from it took a stack of prints. He put them on the table.

They still smelled of darkroom chemicals. "Go on," he said. "Take a look."

47.

I can't tell you what I felt when I saw those pictures, Doctor: the sickness and the sadness, the depths of the depravity. There were a dozen or more prints showing Marilyn on the floor of Chalet 52 crawling around, just lying there or wallowing, blasted out of her mind. Wasted.

According to Billy, when Sinatra saw the pictures, he said, "They're pretty sick, aren't they?" And Billy said, "Yes, they are. *Really* sick."

"What do you think I ought to do with them?" Sinatra asked, and Billy said, "Burn them."

"Did you make any copies?" he asked.

"No," Billy lied.

I see the photos when I close my eyes, Doc. I can't get them out of my head: Marilyn, sick and moaning under the man who was wearing my shirt—and then wearing nothing at all.

48.

Pucini never advertised. It didn't need to. It was co-owned by Sinatra and Lawford, so it was booked until Doomsday. To get a reservation, first you had to know the Secret Name of God. Not to mention His number. Then you had to call Him. If you happened to finally reach Him, and told Him your name, and asked Him for a reservation, He would put you on hold, look for a pencil, send a flood, burn a bush, and tell you, "No."

The maître d' that night was hardly God, but he acted like it. He took a swift look at me, an almost imperceptible up-and-down that registered everything he needed to know before he smiled thinly and said, "Sir?"

"I'm looking for Jo Carnahan," I said.

Over his shoulders, down the aisle that led to the stage, I saw her sitting on the curved edge of a white booth to the right. She was facing the front door. Her Kool was in a holder, and she gestured with it as she spoke; smoking was a form of punctuation for her. She smoked the way other people use commas. The diamonds that hung like teardrops from her ears sparkled in the light from the high chandeliers.

Lawrence Welk and his Champagne Orchestra played on the

stage you could see past the cigarette girls, like French maids, who roamed the aisle between two rows of banquettes.

"That's her," I said, pushing the maître d' aside and walking toward the tables.

"I'm afraid you can't—"

It turned out I couldn't: I stopped when, around the pane of leaded glass that obscured part of Jo's table, I saw the man.

Captain James Hamilton of the LAPD was a drinking buddy of Chief William Parker; they'd worked together in Army Intelligence during the war. In civilian life, Hamilton started out as chief investigator for the police commission, but—like Hoover—he was secretly conducting investigations *of* the police commission . . . and reporting what he'd learned about his colleagues back to then–deputy chief Parker.

Hamilton used surveillance (Fred Otash, Bernie Spindel) to eliminate and intimidate his enemies. And when he torpedoed Parker's rival, Thad Brown, Parker promoted Hamilton to captain and chief of the Gangster Squad, or the Intelligence Division.

But under Hamilton, the Intelligence Division didn't seem so interested in the bad guys: Hamilton and Parker wanted to know where film star bodies were buried, which studs were flits, which starlets were lezbos, who'd fucked whom, who liked little boys, who drank too much, and whose arms were studded with needle tattoos.

Hamilton was Bobby Kennedy's favorite cop. Back when he'd been a member of the Kefauver Commission, Bobby had operated out of Hamilton's office while in L.A., and Hamilton turned his own best men into Bobby's drivers, valets, and security guards.

So I didn't walk over to Jo. Instead, I fired up a Kent and found a seat at the bar by the window and hung my hat on the hook. I ordered Wild Turkey from the man behind the bar in his black jacket with a shirt and a tie that was almost as red as his nose. His hair shone blue with oil.

"Waiting for a date?" the bartender asked.

"You could say that," I said. "Actually, I wonder if you could send a note to a friend: just a note on a napkin to a lady across the room?"

"Of course, sir. Where is she?"

"She's the woman in white ermine at Captain Hamilton's table," I said. Then, on a napkin, I wrote "Miss Carnahan: phone call for you from Delilah."

And when one of the efficient, white-jacketed waiters arrived at the bar with a silver tray, the barkeep handed him the folded napkin. "Table fifteen," he said.

I lit another cigarette and watched through the smoke as Jo read the note, leaned to the side, and looked toward the front desk. Her eyes were round and she was white, but she hadn't seen me. She daubed her lips with a napkin and said something to Captain Hamilton, then stood and adjusted her ermine. She walked (I would say glided) down the aisle through the tables to the front desk.

Her face fell when she saw me. "Ben."

"I need to talk to you."

"You can't be here. What if he sees me with—"

"There's a parking lot in back."

You are having problems with the tape again. Or at least it seems that way; the fact is that the eleventh reel is finished. It is time for the twelfth. You remove it from the Sony, mark the cardboard box with my name and the number eleven, then spool the new tape onto the reels, hitting PLAY, then REWIND, and PLAY.

Finally, you hit RECORD, smile up at me and, as if giving an orchestra their cue, say, "Five, four, three, two—"

"All that bullshit about investigative journalism," I said outside, "but what ends up in your column is trick-golf shots and Bob Hope. You weren't investigating a story, Jo: You were investigating *me*. For your boyfriend."

"You don't understand." She was beginning to cry. "I wish I could make you—"

"You knew I was at Verona. You *told* him. That's why he showed up—"

She pulled away. I slapped her.

"—pretending to be Johnny."

"Ben—"

"Let me tell you something about your handsome captain, Jo," I said, shaking her shoulders. "He raped Miss Monroe. They drugged her and took pictures. It was blackmail. They wanted the diary."

"No. They wanted the tape."

"What?"

"I want you to see someone," she whispered. "His name is Fred Otash. Ask him about Rock Hudson."

She opened her purse and took out her pen and was writing something in her reporter's notebook when I heard the captain's voice: "Jo!"

I turned.

Captain Hamilton stood, a bantam barrel of a man, by the Dumpsters at the door leading out from the kitchen. His right arm was in a sling. I probably don't need to tell you he'd been shot by Johnny, Doc. The point is that he wore a bespoke suit—pocket square, pearl tie pin, pocket watch with gold chain. Drill-sergeant eyes popped from pink skin scrubbed to a raw sheen. Maybe the eyes had started out as blue but now looked boiled, like pale pearl onions in a gimlet glass. His crew cut made it impossible to tell if his hair was gray or blond, but bristles of hair jutted from the rolls of red skin on his neck.

"What have we here?" he said. "A little backdoor tête-à-tête."

"Hello, James," Jo said. "This is—"

"Ah, don't tell me: the fabled Delilah!" I smelled gin and Hai Karate as he stepped toward me. "So you're the bastard who's been stealing my clothes."

49.

The Champagne Orchestra was playing "Tiny Bubbles" as Captain Hamilton escorted Jo and me to his banquette near the stage. It was covered in a white cloth, red candle in the center, the ravaged remains of dinner—lobster Newburg, steak béarnaise—sitting on the uncleared plates beside the napkins and the baskets filled with breadsticks.

The banquette was a padded white half-moon around which two other couples sat:

Steve McQueen and Neile Adams.

Red Buttons and Helayne McNorton.

"Now," Captain Hamilton said as I sat between him and Jo on the curved booth that faced the front door, "I suggest we all get to know each other. Everyone, this is a friend of Jo's. A very, shall we say, *good* friend of Jo's. And, as I'm so fond of saying, any friend of Jo's is a friend of mine." He turned to Jo. "Darling, make the introductions."

Nervously, she said, "Ben Fitzgerald, this is Captain James Hamilton."

"We've met," I said.

"Steve McQueen and Neile."

"Nice to meet you."

"Oh, sure."

"And Red Buttons and Helayne."

"Now," Captain Hamilton said, "you were saying, Jo darling."

"Sorry?"

"When I stepped outside, I found you and this . . . *friend* speaking. You said, 'Rock Hudson.' "

"*James.*" Jo smiled. "You've had too much to drink."

"I asked a question."

"If the lady doesn't feel like talking—"

"Mind your business, Delilah, and I'll mind mine."

"Very well then." She broke into her Annie Laurie voice: "What Hollywood Heartthrob's's shrinker told his wife that the snakes he saw in inkblots meant the male penis, dear ones?"

"Really, Jo—"

"Seems this Giant of a film star had an affair with a married male friend, then went to the man's house and had dinner with the man's wife. Surely Heaven does not Allow that! He had an affair with his very own agent in Palm Springs. His Magnificent Obsession? Picking up boys on Santa Monica Boulevard."

"You saying Rock Hudson is a queer?" Steve asked.

"I'm a reporter, darling."

"You're goddamn Annie Laurie," said the captain. "And that is the most ridiculous thing I've ever heard."

"—quest," Lawrence Welk said from the stage. "Captain Hamilton?"

The blue spotlight turned to Captain Hamilton. Steve McQueen and Red Buttons smiled, then clapped.

"We're taking requests," Lawrence Welk said. "What-a would-a you-a like to hear?"

"Nothing. I don't want to hear nothing."

Jo slipped a piece of paper over my left thigh.

The captain noticed: "What—?"

I grabbed the paper and raised my hand. The spotlight spun to me.

"*You*, then, sir."

I blinked.

"What's your request?"

I said the first thing I could remember, the first thing out of my mouth, which was—

"'Young World,'" Lawrence Welk said. "The Ricky Nelson hit, sung by the lovely and talented Miss Kitty Wells. Miss Kitty, please invite Mr. Fitzgerald up to sing with you."

The next thing I knew I was onstage looking down the aisle flanked by the white booths and all those minks and martinis, standing beside Kitty as Lawrence Welk said, "A-one an' a-two."

I couldn't remember the words, and though the spotlight blinded me, I kept thinking I saw Jo with tears in her eyes, mouthing the lyrics that I had forgotten as Lawrence Welk danced with the "Champagne Lady."

Applause.

I squinted into the light, bowing, watching Steve and Red and Jo clapping. The captain didn't clap.

He was waiting for me to return.

But I did not. I bowed and waved and ducked past the low podiums behind which the musicians sat in powder-blue tuxedos and slipped around the cyclorama into the back stage filled with wires, and heard Lawrence strike up "Bubbles in the Wine" as I pushed through the kitchen, and out into the parking lot.

50.

Might want to pace yourself," the bartender said. "The night is young."

"The night was young five years ago, maybe."

"The night is as young as you want it to be. And as long. If you keep drinking."

"Amen to that," I said. I was canceling time like a ticket, pulling hands from the face of the clock. I didn't want the time.

I didn't need it.

The bar along the left wall was festooned with colored Christmas lights and stained with what remained of powdered snow sprayed around the mirror, against which rows of bright bottles and a heavy cash register sat. The bar itself was long and dotted with coasters and empties and a catsup bottle, a few napkin holders, a hurricane lamp, and plastic ashtrays from other bars in other, better parts of town.

After maybe the fifth shot, I told myself, *I'm done now*—and meant it—but there were all those sirens in the night. This was the rationale. I suppose there are always sirens, but *that* night I was sure they were for me. The clothes that I was wearing belonged to L.A.'s chief of police; the monogram on the pocket was his, and he knew I was in love with his mistress.

"You ever," I said, "been with a woman who lied to you?"

"Is there any other kind? I mean since Eve?"

"Guess not."

"She break your heart?"

"They *both* did," I said.

I woke the next morning in the back of my car parked in a lot fringed with weeds that had grown over the fence. It had rained in the night and the rutted tracks in the dirt were filled with water. You probably wonder how I ended up out there. It wasn't just that I was drunk. The fact is I couldn't go home. Remember how Jo had seen lights in my hotel? (Sorry, Doc: *apartment.*) Well, they'd been there when I returned "home" from the bar last night, too. No one had been in the lobby; the bar had been closed, and my key hadn't worked in my lock.

So I ended up out *here*, feeling springs in my back.

I wiped crumbs from my eyes and dried spit from the edges of my mouth and opened the back door and walked to the front. I pulled my pockets inside out, revealing bar napkins with scrawled messages and numbers so confusing they might as well have been Sanskrit. Change fell, too, along with my keys and the paper Jo had slipped me:

"Fred Otash Detective Bureau," it read, "1342 Laurel."

WEDNESDAY, AUGUST 22

51.

It was Rock Hudson's voice that I heard on the Sony tape in Otash's office. I would have known it anywhere. I had seen most of his movies, had always thought of him as a man's man. But I guess I'm going on the record now as saying that, if anything, Rock Hudson was a man's woman. And not just one man's. Almost every man's.

On the tape his wife said, "You told Christine that you had found great happiness in your homosexuality."

"I don't know why I said that. Because I haven't. You know there was Jack. [unintelligible] That was unhappy."

"And then there was Randy."

"Oh, yes."

"Don't you learn by your mistakes?"

"Yes. Everyone does, for God's sake."

"Then why do you continue to do it, over and over? I know everything. I know why I didn't hear from you in Italy, and what you were doing before Italy, and since you got back."

Otash stopped the reel-to-reel and smiled, his cigar extended between fat fingers studded with oversized rings.

I never understood why they call a face a *mug* until I met Fred Otash. His face was half jowls and half eyes. His eyes were black and they followed you even when his head did not, like Jesus in paintings. He wore paisley shirts open at his wide collar, his chest hair matching his white sideburns.

"So that's how it's done," he said. "The wife hired me to tape him as part of the divorce. There are others. They hire me, and I get in'air. Sometimes I have to get in'air without the whole house knowing, so someone who works for me dresses up like a plumber or something and the truck that's parked outside reads 'Twenty-four-Hour TV Repair' or 'Roofing Company' or 'Furniture Company.' My favorite is 'Otash Plumbing: We Clean Cesspools.' "

"Boy, do you ever," I said.

"A man's gotta live."

"Do you do electricity?"

"I don't know what you mean?"

"Are you ever B. F. Fox?"

"Never heard of it," he said, but I wasn't so sure.

"Why?" you ask me now. "Did you think he bugged the Savoy?"

I nod. "I had seen him before, Doc."

"Where?"

"In the Monroe house," I say. "The night I broke in."

His office was in West Hollywood between Sunset and Santa Monica. It wasn't far from the Hollywood Hills. There had been fires in Cajon Pass the night before and I could smell the smoke through the window that overlooked the fire escape and the gray brick walls and shaded windows of the nearby building. I saw a pair of binoculars on the sill under the spotted window. The spots on the window were dead flies.

Otash hit PLAY again.

The Hudson tape continued, and I heard the star confess that, while in Italy filming *A Farewell to Arms*, he engaged in an affair with an "Italian member of the crew, Roberto or Francis or something, a most discreet man." I heard the wife telling Rock that the doctor knew his problems by his "inkblots," she said. "You told me you saw thousands of butterflies and also snakes. Butterflies mean femininity, and snakes represent the male penis. . . . There isn't anything glandular about your homosexuality, it is only a freezing at an emotional state, and it's up to the individual to grow out of it."

But he didn't. He had an affair with a married male friend, then went to the man's house and had dinner with the man and his wife. He had an affair with his predatory agent, Henry Willson, a "bitch in heat" (the wife said) in Palm Springs. And "everyone knows you were picking up boys off the street shortly after we were married," she said. "People don't talk if you aren't doing anything. You never hear these stories about Gary Cooper."

Otash hit STOP. "So," he said. "Now you know what I do. You going to tell me why you're here?"

"Jo sent me."

"I know that."

"She said there was a tape."

"What tape?"

"She said that you knew Marilyn."

"Oh, Jesus, not this—"

"What's 'this'?"

"I guess you know," he said, "if you know Jo."

You've heard of Peter Lawford, Doc—the boozy English actor who had, through good graces and looks, insinuated himself into the Kennedy family by marrying the president's sister, Pat, in 1954. Sinatra had famously dubbed him the Brother-in-Lawford, though people forget now that Kennedy himself was first known as the guy whose sister was married to the movie star. What you might not know is that the beach house Lawford bought, the old Louis B. Mayer mansion in Santa Monica, became a sort of White House West—the place where the president relaxed in Los Angeles. It was, as such, a presidential whorehouse.

"There were parties," Otash said, chewing his cigar. "*Extreme* ones."

When Pat was away, Peter stocked the house with starlets and would-be singers, waitresses and child acrobats, girls who did nothing but walk around in bikinis with thumbs in their mouths, girls who sat stoned and nude with legs spread on the edges of beds. There was music and booze, and when the orgies ended, often around dawn, the president would take one or two of his favorite "kids" back to his hotel.

That is why the house had bugs: "And I don't mean cockroaches," Otash said. "*Four* bugs were installed. In the bedroom, on the phones. Numerous tapes were made of Marilyn and Jack in the act of love."

"Did you hear Bobby Kennedy on a tape, too?"

"Yes."

"At the Lawford house?"

"The *Monroe* house."

"There were bugs in the Brentwood hacienda?"

"Yes."

"Did the tapes confirm that Bobby and Marilyn had an affair?"

"Of course . . . sure. Bobby and Marilyn were recorded many times."

"Were tapes recorded at Marilyn's house up until her death?"

"They were recorded on the day of her death . . . the *night* of her death."

"A conversation with Kennedy?"

"*Bobby* Kennedy."

"And what were they talking about?"

"It was a violent argument. She was saying, 'I feel passed around! I feel used! I feel like a piece of meat!' "

"And you heard this tape?"

"One of them."

"One."

"There were two. One belonged to the Kennedys."

"And the second?"

"It was Marilyn's. They've torn that place upside down trying to find it. That's why there was a delay before anyone was called."

"They didn't find it?"

"They wondered if I knew where it was. I didn't. I would have told them. The only one who thinks she knows for sure is Jeanne Carmen."

"And what does Jeanne Carmen say?"

"Marilyn hid it in a bus locker."

"Well, that should tell you something."

"You know how many bus lockers there are in this city, guy?"

52.

882 North Doheny Drive is a triplex on the corner of Cynthia Street. Sinatra's accountant manages the place, which is why the singer's secretary lives there. So does Jeanne Carmen, who had more than once been the willing if not eager recipient of the Chairman of the Board's affections, which were as changeable as the weather in San Francisco, where both he and Tony Bennett had so glibly left their hearts. Marilyn herself had first lived at Doheny before she married DiMaggio. She moved back after divorcing the playwright. She stayed there, a kind of way station, on her way to the permanent digs—as permanent as her digs would ever be. She died only six months after moving to Brentwood.

But you know that already.

So do I.

What I didn't know was what Jeanne Carmen knew, or had been led to believe, about the tape.

I went in through the lobby. The bell didn't work, so I stood by the mailboxes smoking before someone emerged, a woman with her dog, and I climbed three flights to 3A, the alphanumeric I had found next to the initials J.C. on the mailbox.

I knocked.

A voice: "Hang on a second."

A dog barked—one of those precious teacups that use noise to overcompensate for the fact that they can only shake and pee. Jeanne opened the door three fingers and peered out. She wore a bathrobe. Her blond hair was mussed. Roots peeked from the scalp, looking vaguely skunkish. She wore no makeup. I wondered if she'd been up all night. Maybe I had woken her.

"Who are you?"

I tipped my hat. "Ben Fitzgerald, ma'am. Friend of Jo Carnahan's."

"What are you doing here?"

"We met at Ciro's. You said I looked like Don Taylor, ma'am. You said Shakespeare—"

"Get out of here."

"You said Shakespeare said 'more's the pity.' "

"Shakespeare said a lot of things. It's no concern of mine."

She started to close the door. I put my foot in it. "If I could just have a minute of your time."

"You already *had* a minute."

"One more, then. One question, really."

She opened the door slightly.

"You told Miss Carnahan about a tape."

"I don't remember."

"You know Jo Carnahan."

"Socially."

"You said Marilyn had a tape."

"Who said anything about a tape?"

"Jo, ma'am. She said—"

"That bitch."

A voice from inside: "Jeanne?" A man. Was this one of her pill parties? Or was she entertaining one of her extracurriculars? "Who is it?" he asked.

"Wrong number," she said, and closed the door.

Sure, a Big Story was out there somewhere in our sprawling, sports-starved metropolis just waiting for Benjamin Fitzgerald, deputy coroner, to break it. But a guy can get discouraged—especially when he hasn't eaten in twenty-four hours.

So I ordered the ham and eggs at the first restaurant I could find, an evil place where I discovered mold on the bottom of the pie that I wanted just to tide me over before the eggs. The old woman behind the counter didn't seem to have washed her hair. Her hairnet looked like a clogged drain. That should have tipped me off. I didn't want the eggs anymore—they were probably filled with shells or blood—so I canceled my order.

She handed me the bill, but when I reached into my wallet I realized I had nothing left. "Look, I have to get money."

"Oldest trick in the book."

"I don't have money, ma'am. But I can leave my hat."

"It's not much of a hat. Not worth the price of that pie."

"That pie was garbage."

"I *made* that pie."

"There's mold on the bottom."

"That isn't mold," she said. "It's tapioca."

"—overdrawn," said the bank manager. "We've been trying to contact you. We're quite troubled about checks made out for an inordinate amount of money, and have no choice but to close—"

"I didn't *write* any checks."

"Let's not drift down this tiresome route, Mr. Fitzgerald. Trust me: I've traveled it often. It has been a trying day and I have all but exhausted my patience. We've been trying to contact you."

"I've been on vacation."

"That's not what we heard."

"Oh?"

"We tracked you down at work," he said. "They said that you were fired."

53.

Taking everything into account, what action, if any, do you think the U.S. should take at this time in regard to Cuba?

Bomb, invade . . . 10%

Trade embargo . . . 13%

Something short of war . . . 26%

Hands off . . . 22%

Other action . . . 4%

Don't know . . . 23%

I don't know, either, Doc. No one does. I am reading the Gallup poll results in the *Times* as you try to make the Sony work. It has stopped again. When it finally kicks in, you stare at the turning tape, sweat beading on your forehead as you light another cigarette and say, "Put the paper down."

I do.

"Now continue."

"Where were we?" I manage a yawn.

"You went to pay for the pie. You didn't have the money."

"Worse," I said. "I didn't have a job."

I returned to the place where I had spent my adult working life, the rat's labyrinth of dark halls and empty offices, and heard the giggling just before I saw the man with a brush. He was repainting the name on my office door. My name had been removed; it was now nothing but a splotch that lay, along with my postcard from the Pick-Carter in Cleveland, on the papers that covered the floor.

"'Scuse me." I said.

The painter turned to me.

"This is my office," I said.

"So why is Archie in there?"

I heard the giggling again. Through the half-opened door, I saw feet on a desk. They began to jiggle as the man named Archie whispered, then laughed again.

I stepped inside.

He was nuzzling the phone, his broad grin stretching over most of his face. His right hand was cupped over the receiver and mouth. I stood until he caught my eye, put his hand on the receiver, and said, "May I help you?"

"What are you doing here?"

"Just working."

"Working."

"The daily grind. All that. Another day, another three-fifty an hour. And all that."

"I mean what are you doing *here*?"

"Oh, here."

"My office."

"Yours?" He looked around, surprised. "What's your name?"

"Ben Fitzgerald."

"Oh, hey, Ben. Tell me: How are your 'other opportunities' going?"

"What?"

"The ones you 'left' to 'pursue.'"

"I don't follow."

"The memo said you left LACCO 'to pursue other opportunities.' In Cleveland."

"Who said Cleveland?"

"Who else?" he said. "Curphey."

I found him on the sixth hole, a bunker cut within the putting surface of the Riviera Country Club, built over the sets that director Thomas Ince had constructed on the slopes of the Santa Ynez Canyon in 1912. Back then, it was known as Inceville, where the director made hundreds of movies that no one remembers now. You could walk through ersatz Japanese villages, Puritan settlements, and Swiss streets seven miles up the hills from the spot where Sunset ends at the Pacific Coast Highway. The place only lasted ten years. The first fire hit in 1916. By 1922 it was already a ghost town.

Now it's the Pacific Palisades.

"Dr. Curphey?" I said.

He stopped, looked up, and turned. He was smoking his pipe. "Ben."

"I want to speak with you."

"Another time."

"Was I fired?"

"I *said* another time."

I grabbed the club from his hands. "I went on vacation like you told me to go on vacation and I forgot what you told me to forget but I came back to the office this morning to find that someone had taken my job."

"Archie didn't *take* your job," Curphey said. "He *earned* it. He's a hardworking, *moral* young man. That's what we need in this office."

"I perjured myself for you."

"And you stole a diary from the Monroe house. And you stole Nembutals from the Monroe file. And you stole the key to the Evidence Room. Now we asked you to get help."

"I was never offered help."

"You turned it down."

"I don't have a job. What am I supposed to do?"

"I'm sure you're familiar with the classifieds. I suggest you check them out. Now, please give me my club."

"I have a son to support."

"Oh? I hear he's being supported by a gangster. Who happens to be fucking your wife."

I swung the iron straight into Curphey's crotch. The pipe popped from his mouth, ashes burning on the kikuyu grass. He staggered backward with an "oof," clutching his groin even as I felt the hands grab me from behind: one guy on each side as they dragged me, kicking, down the fairway.

You can see the pictures, Doc. They show me struggling, maybe even "drunk." Well, that's the power of suggestion. But if someone handed you them and said, "He was drunk and disorderly," wouldn't you agree?

It sure looks that way.

Lots of things do.

"And that was when it hit me," I say.

"What?"

"Curphey said I'd stolen the key to the Evidence Room."

"So?"

"It was true," I say. "And I still had it."

54.

Rewind, Doc, to the point in the tape where I first entered the Evidence Room, carrying the log that Carl had given me:

CASE NO.: 81128

DECEDENT NAME: Marilyn Monroe

CONTENTS:

1. **A vial of 25 Nembutal capsules from San Vicente Pharmacy**
2. **A vial of ten chloral hydrate tablets filled on July 25**
3. **A small key with a red plastic cover labeled "15"**
4. **The water glass**

LOCATION: Box 24, Row 13-B

I wanted No. 3. I knew what it was *for* now. So I went back to LACCO, unlocked the Sheriff's Evidence Room with that first purloined key, and opened the box. I removed the small red key, left Pneumonia Hall, and drove back out to Brentwood, where I waited for the sun to fall. At 8:51, I parked in the cul-de-sac and walked under the dark jacarandas down Sixth to another cul-de-sac. There was a locked gate to the right. It fronted on a driveway. I vaulted over it, walked along the strip of land between the driveway and another house, and all the way back to Miss Monroe's pool.

I walked left along the narrow lawn to the window of the room where she had died. I pulled myself up and dropped down.

At the end of the hall, I stepped into the living room. The furniture had been removed. Nothing was left, not even the feeling you sometimes get from empty houses—a lingering sense of the energy that had once existed. It was a battery without juice, the husk of an orange in a garbage can.

But the mail was there. The post office had kept delivering it. They always do. It was under the door:

A bill from I. Magnin's, a bill from BankAmericard, a letter from someone named "Peters," and (last) an envelope from the Greyhound Bus Station in North Hollywood.

I opened the Greyhound envelope, a federal offense. But everything I had done recently was some kind of offense. And they were going to kill me anyway.

Inside I found a bill for bus locker #15.

The light was low, the place gray and airless. Sad army posters peeled from the walls, and vending machines with chocolate bars that had seen better days were tethered to the wall sockets by mouse-eaten cords. The few conscious souls who prowled the station at this hour (Mexican convicts and tea freaks, wasted girls with sullen come-ons who trailed strands of bleached hair like an army of balding Rapunzels) moved like some sentient species of sea plankton.

I walked to the long wall of lockers, put the key in #15, and found what I was looking for.

55.

Amahl and the Night Visitors is a one-act opera by Gian Carlo Menotti. It's a Christmas classic, the first opera composed specifically for TV, broadcast live on NBC's *Hallmark Hall of Fame* on Christmas Eve, 1951. It was inspired by Hieronymus Bosch's painting *The Adoration of the Magi*, which Menotti saw on a trip to the Metropolitan Museum of Art in—

"What does that have to do with anything?" you ask.

I point to the evidence:

5. *Amahl and the Night Visitors*

"So?"

"It's what I found at Colony Records."

"Why did you go to Colony Records?"

"It was the only place that I could think of that would have a reel-to-reel."

The store was on La Cienega near Sunset, a labyrinth of walls stocked with dusty used records (*The Music Man*); plastic-wrapped new ones (101 Strings, Bill Cosby); and rows of reel-to-reel tapes. *Amahl and the Night Visitors* was playing when I walked in, the man with the clipped Vandyke behind the front counter closing his eyes as he conducted the unseen orchestra with a pencil.

"Excuse me," I said.

He looked up.

I showed him the Sony tape I had found in the bus locker. "I really want to hear this," I said, "and wondered if—"

"We're already listening."

"But it's Henry Mancini."

That seemed to comfort him.

At first my tape was filled with odd sounds—clicking and indistinct. Hangers jangling in a closet. Laughter and someone talking in a vague way on the phone. But it wasn't long before I heard the unmistakable sound of sex.

"That isn't 'Moon River,'" the manager said.

"No."

"It's not 'Baby Elephant Walk,' either." He turned the tape off. "I think you had better leave."

From the envelope you now remove a series of photos, each showing a close-up of a man's terrified face, each more savage and brutal than the last.

"Why did you beat up the photographer?" you ask.

"I didn't."

"When you left Colony Records, you saw Duane Mikkelson sitting in a car, and you beat him to a pulp."

"I didn't."

"Well, *someone* did," you say. "If it wasn't you—"

It's true that, when I left the store, I saw the car across the street. I walked to it and stared through the window at Mikkelson's grinning mouth. It's true that I pulled him out onto the street. It's true that I threw him onto the ground, put my shoe under his chin, and told him to drop the camera.

"You sonnavabitch," he said. "Cheating on your wife."

"I never cheated—"

"The camera doesn't lie."

"But cameramen do."

From the cars around us, four men emerged in dungarees and plaid shirts. The first was the same psychopathically grinning Jimmy Cagney with the porkpie hat I had seen at Triple XXX. He stood with the three others, Irish thugs who looked ready to plant me in the pavement—but they picked up Mikkelson instead, and hung him in the air from the back of his suit like a scarecrow. His feet kicked, swimming in nothing, as Cagney slammed his fist into the shutterbug's nose—and another man grabbed hold of the camera.

Blood.

"Hey!" Mikkelson said. "I *work* for you guys."

Flash!

This went on until he could hardly speak, his face the pulpy tomato you see here in the pictures.

Now you ask: "What did he mean by 'I work for you guys'?"

"He meant LAPD."

"How do *you* know?"

Captain Hamilton stepped out from one of the cars. He took the tape and the diary and then arrested me: "For assault and battery," he said.

"Don't get fresh," I said as Cagney patted down my pants.

"He's a comedian, see," the captain said. "Hey, comedian. Ever hear the joke about the man who beat up a photographer?"

"No."

"He went to jail," he said, opening my wallet. "Where's your license?"

"In my wallet."

"All I see is this." He handed me the Get Out of Jail Free card. "It won't work. You go to jail. Go directly to jail. Do not pass go—"

56.

I did not collect two hundred dollars.

I was cuffed and searched in the hall on the concrete against the red wall; they patted me down and removed my property, putting my belt and shoes in plastic bags. They even took my socks off. They took the handcuffs off and patted me down again, face hard against the wall.

"You liked frisking me so much, you had to do it a second time?" I asked.

"Yeah," one cop said. "And your sister was there, too."

I waited to be booked in the holding tank. I waited for I wasn't sure how long, until—

In the Booking Area, the jailer stood behind a desk against cheap wood paneling. On the desk was a typewriter.

They took my fingerprints on an ink pad on a small shitty table near the desk. They took my photo from two angles, front and side. My booking number was displayed on a metal rectangular box that extended, like a sideways T, from a galvanized pole. The jailer loosened it with a screw, moving it up to just under my chin.

"Name?" the jailer asked.

"Ben Fitzgerald."

"DOB."

"Seven/eleven/twenty-nine."

"Occupation."

"Deputy coroner, Suicide Notes and Weapons. Or, well, it used to be."

"Used to?"

"I'm not sure it's my job anymore."

"Unemployed," he said. "Sex?"

"What do you think?"

"Yeah, and your sister was there, too. *Sex?*"

"Male."

"Height."

"Five foot eleven inches."

"Any medical conditions?"

"No."

The jailer typed all this on the form. I signed it. The bail was preset. They let me make one phone call. I called Verona Gardens:

"Rose," I said. "It's Ben. I'm calling from—"

"That hotel?"

"Worse. I only have five minutes. Max okay?"

"What is this about?"

"I need help."

"Jesus."

"I'm in jail. I can explain."

"Ben."

"I need bail."

"You think I have the money?"

"You're dating Johnny. He's a mobster. Maybe he could peel off some of that Monopoly money and head on over to the—"

"He's not *that* kind of mobster."

"What other kind *is* there?"

"I really have to go."

"Time's up," the man said.

There were five male Felony cells with heavy old bars in the jail. Mine was 10 × 10 and had a toilet, a sink, a mirror, and a bed. They gave me a bag of hygiene supplies (toothbrush, soap, and a towel) and locked me in.

So I waited and I smoked. I don't know how much time passed. All I knew was that the pile of butts kept growing. It was like *this* place, Doc. There were no windows; the only light came from the bare bulb on the ceiling.

They slipped the *Mirror* under the cell door. In it, I found an item about a man named Ben Fitzgerald, a former member of the Los Angeles County Coroner's Office who, drunk and disorderly, had beaten a photographer and was now being held on bail in the Men's Central Jail on Bauchet:

> Fitzgerald's wife recently filed for divorce on account of "physical and mental cruelty" and is living in seclusion with their son because, sources say, she is "afraid for her life."

At some point the guard slipped a tray of food under the cell door. I stared at the congealed Salisbury steak and the cup of soup, a small carton of milk smelling like the refrigerator. I wasn't hungry. I let the tray sit and stretched out on the bed.

In the middle of the night—or what *seemed* like night—I woke to the sound of scraping. Two rats were eating the food that I had left behind.

In the morning, they were dead.

The guard was unlocking the door. "Rise and shine," he said. "Someone paid your bail, mister."

"Rose?"

"No," he said. "Your brother."

THURSDAY, AUGUST 23

57.

I don't have a brother, but this is what I knew about my "brother," Doc: He drank a quart of Scotch and smoked four packs of cigarettes a day. He spent Hollywood nights in a Caddy filled with girls he called his "Little Sweeties." He'd been an LAPD dick for ten years but ran afoul of Chief William Parker so went out on his own as a private eye. But when he was convicted of doping a horse at Santa Anita, his license was suspended. That didn't stop him, though.

He just went underground.

His face was half jowls and half eyes. I'm repeating myself, but listen: His eyes were black and they followed you even when his head did not, like Jesus in paintings. He wore paisley shirts open at his wide collar, his chest hair matching his white sideburns. My brother looked a lot like Fred Otash.

That's because he *was* Fred Otash.

Now you tell me that I'm crazy: "This is beginning to sound like paranoid schizophrenia."

"Come on."

"A common delusion among schizos is that they're being singled out for harm—the government is taping their phone calls or a coworker is poisoning their coffee or they are being stalked by a master wiretapper who shows up at the jail and pretends to be their brother."

"But he *did*."

"Sure," you say. "See what I mean?"

"Heya, brother," Fred said.

"I don't *have* a brother."

"He gets like this," Fred said to the guard. "Goes through phases and all. It's getting worse. I don't know what to do."

"Take care of him, huh?"

"Sure," Fred said. "It's what I'm here for."

"He's gonna kill me," I said.

Fred shot the guard another sad look.

"Best of luck, buddy," the guard said.

He left us alone.

Fred took the Smith & Wesson from under his jacket and held it to my gut. "Are you ready to behave?"

I didn't respond.

"Say 'yes,' baby brother."

"Yes."

"Good." He kissed me on the forehead. "I'm sure you know why I'm here."

"I have an idea."

"A tape. A Sony reel-to-reel."

"Captain Hamilton took it."

"But the tape he took was not the tape you found. I'm sure you can imagine the surprise when we played it for some powerful people, brother, who were wakened in the night to hear an *opera*."

"An opera."

. . .

Now you turn your tape off and remove another from Evidence: Item No. 5. You thread its brown strands into the take-up reel, REWIND, FAST FORWARD, and PLAY:

"Oh Mother!" a boy soprano sings. ". . . There's never been such a sky—"

You hit STOP. *"Amahl and the Night Visitors,"* you say. You light another cigarette, drag, and blow smoke in a stream to the ceiling.

"You never know what you might find in a bus station locker after midnight," I say.

"I know what you found in the bus station locker after midnight, Ben, and it was not Gian Carlo Menotti's one-act opera. Now for the last time—"

"Where's the tape?" Fred asked.

"I don't know."

"I don't believe you."

"I don't give a shit."

"Oh, really?" He reached inside his pocket, withdrawing a small purple dinosaur:

The Toy Surprise.

"You son of a bitch."

"Hey, it's swell to see you, kid," he said. "It's been a while. Now, let's talk about old times."

He led me from the jail. Out the front door, we stepped straight into a camera crew, the TV lights flooding my eyes.

"Good evening, dear ones," Jo said. "This is Annie Laurie."

58.

We drove out to Point Dume. I'd always thought it was spelled "Doom." That day it might as well have been. It was nice in Jo's DeSoto with the top down, the wind in her hair and kerchief, her sunglasses on though it was overcast. The city vanished as we followed the PCH, past shuttered nightclubs along the cliffs and the crashing waves that I could hear but only vaguely saw in the haze that led out to the horizon.

"Where are we going?"

"A place I know. In Malibu."

"Why?"

"You have to ask? They're after you."

It started to rain. She put the top up. I turned the radio dial until I found a working station.

"Not Ricky Nelson," she said.

"I *like* Ricky Nelson."

"Something else."

"You know the words to 'Young World.' I saw you singing them." She took a drag. The ash crackled. "Cigarette?"

"No thanks. I quit."

"Since when?"

"This morning."

"You liar."

"Coming from you," I said, "that's rich. Don't you think you have a lot of explaining to do?"

"How much time do you have?"

"Don't answer a question with a question."

I don't remember everything she said, Doctor, but I remember that she said she'd met Captain James Hamilton in 1959 while following a lead: *Dragnet*'s Jack Webb had asked LAPD's Captain Parker to use his bug man, Phelps, to spy on Webb's former wife, Julie London.

Captain Hamilton took Jo to drinks at the Villa Capri to convince her to lay off Webb, the LAPD's PR puppy. Over martinis and cigars, in exchange for keeping quiet in her column about Webb, he gave her scandal-sheet stuff about Liberace's trouser-chasing and Robert Mitchum's pot-smoking as his hand slipped under her skirt, a brush meant not for her skin but for his. Still, she twitched in a way that indicated it was not altogether unwelcome.

It wasn't unwelcome for years.

"He kept saying he would leave his wife but never did," she said. "They never do. I wasn't sure I wanted it anyway. What we had was special—it wasn't mundane. No one took the garbage out. No one nagged about feeding the cats."

"You don't *have* cats."

"That's not the point. He called it The Iron Rules of Love: We would never have birthdays or anniversaries; we could never celebrate, but so? We didn't have the boring, nagging details and chores that collect around love like barnacles, and make it sink."

"Some metaphor."

"Take it or leave it. And things were good. Until."

"What."

"He wanted me to follow you. He threatened me. But everything ended last night."

His wife was out of town, she said. His son was sleeping in the bedroom. He beat Jo up and left her on the bedroom floor. In the middle of the night, she walked down the hall to the living room where the captain sat, an empty glass in hand, passed out on the couch.

Beside him lay the Monroe diary.

"The diary?" I said.

"I have it, Ben."

59.

The water had left a green circle around the drain in the bathroom of the Malibu motel. The pipes shrieked when you turned the faucets on. A torn piece of suicide note or love letter floated on the surface of the water that still ran in the toilet. I removed the cover and pulled the chain and stopped the water running, but behind the shower curtain it still dripped.

We were in the bathroom. She dropped her trench coat, and I saw for the first time the ruined dress with handprints, purple bruises, and the spots of brown that might have been blood on her skin.

"Jesus," I said.

"He was careful not to hit the parts that you can see. That was the important thing. He hit so hard the bottle broke. The bottom ended up on the mantel top," she said, slipping from her clothes.

"I don't want to hurt you."

"You won't." She felt the front of my trousers with the flat of her right hand.

Pearl earrings fell. High heels clattered, too, and torn stockings slipped like Slinkys. The buckled door wouldn't lock, but we shut it. She backed against it, breasts covered with the imprints of my lips on account of the lipstick she had transferred to my face.

I dropped my trousers to my ankles and pushed in. Her body

adjusted, face turned to one side, heart beating in a blue elongated pulse I could see up the side of her neck.

She quoted Lana Turner: "You're my man," she said.

Afterward, we lay side by side on the bed, staring up at the ceiling. We drank Canadian Club from tiny bottles. There were lots of tiny bottles. We'd lit candles, too—some kind of sandalwood that mingled with the smell of surf.

"Let me see the diary," I said.

"Not so fast, Ben."

"That's not what you said twenty minutes ago."

"I didn't *need* to say it twenty minutes ago." I turned my back against her breasts. She folded her arms around my chest. "Let's begin with what we know," she whispered. "What do we know about her last day alive?"

"She seemed happy," I said. "Pat Newcomb spent the night in the Telephone Room. Marilyn spent a sleepless night in her own bedroom, on the phone. In the morning, Marilyn asked for oxygen, the Hollywood cure for a hangover. There wasn't any, so she drank grapefruit juice. She shared it with Newcomb. At some point, she and Pat got into an argument."

"What was the argument about?"

"The fact that Pat had slept all night but Marilyn had not."

"Sure, but why would a woman who never slept begrudge her best friend sleep? A friend she'd invited over? A guest. Did she expect that Newcomb would spend the night awake with her, watching her talk on the phone and pop pills?"

"It doesn't make sense."

"Because it didn't happen," Jo said. "The argument wasn't about sleep."

"What was it about then?"

She stood up and opened her purse.

60.

I've said it before. I'll say it again:

The diary was bound in leather with yellow pages on which blue handwriting had broken all the college rules. The word MEMORIES was embossed on the cover in the same gold that edged the paper. It was a dime-a-dozen diary—available at any drugstore. But now I knew that it could bring down the government. Now I knew that Marilyn had died because of it, and that others would die because of it. It had jeopardized my own life and that of my family. So you ask again: If I had known, would I have just walked away? Let it destroy the girl alone instead of both of us?

I still can't answer that.

I read again the pages I had torn from it:

August 4, 2:01 p.m.

All my hair things in the bag I told you about, the one that I kept in the bathroom: They're gone. I couldn't find them. I told Pat about this, and she said not to worry.

"Don't get so upset," she said.

"Easy for you to say," I said. You who don't have to wake every morning at 5 for a call for a movie that—

That was where it ended. I put this fragment, like a puzzle piece, back inside *The Book of Secrets*, and read:

—no one wants to see on the lot where Whitey is waiting and the whole crew is waiting for me to be beautiful and you don't understand. You just couldn't.

"Mrs. Murray!" But I didn't need to shout since she was there like she came from the shadows like she was watching anyway and always watching. "Yes, Marilyn."

"Have you seen the bag of hair things?"

"No, Marilyn."

Things are going missing all the time now every morning something new has disappeared.

The doorbell rang then. Pat was out by the pool she was still mad. "You can't hold a press conference," she said.

"But sure I can. I'm going to blow this whole thing wide open."

"Marilyn, it's the craziest thing—"

The knock came at the door.

"The General is here," Mrs. Murray said. "With Mr. Lawford."

"Now?"

"Yes."

Well it didn't seem possible he was in San Francisco he never showed up out of nowhere he always called.

"Well, I'm not ready. I don't have my hair things."

"Shall I tell him to go away?"

"Yes."

Diary I went into the bedroom and closed the door. Well, I hadn't slept and everything was over and they told me it was over and the only ones who love me are the guys who sit in the balcony and jerk off. Then there are all those clicks and sounds like someone else on the line once I heard a sort of voice I wonder if [redacted]

I looked at the bottle of pills on the table near the bed and tried to remember how many were there last night I counted them now. Fourteen. I had 14 pills. I looked for the napkin that I'd written notes on near the bed. On the napkin was the number 27 and the name [redacted].

[redacted] got them—

The knock on the door.

"Marilyn?" Mrs. Murray. *"He's outside."*

"Tell him I'm not here."

"He knows you're here."

"Tell him I'm sleeping."

I heard shouting.

"He won't believe you. He's upset. You never sleep. He needs to see you."

"Well, then, tell him to wait. Tell him—"

Here there were two paragraphs of increasingly illegible writing; I could make out only a few words, like "transmitter" and "cordon," until, at the very end of the diary, it became clear again:

> ***A knocking at the door then Mrs. Murray's voice and other voices Bobby and then Peter. I want to fall asleep again want to crawl in bed and disappear. It might be kind of nice to be finished. Now there is another knock and this one at the bedroom.***
>
> ***I wish you would all just leave me alone.***

I closed the diary for the last time and said, "That still doesn't answer the question."

"What question?'

"What was the argument about?"

"You tell *me*, Mr. Mortician."

"I'm not a mortician. I'm a deputy coroner."

"Can't we talk about something less grim?"

"Like what?"

"Us."

"Is that really less grim?"

And in the Long, Deep Sigh Department . . .

She kept quoting Lana Turner.

We finally fell asleep after 2 A.M., the breeze coming over the balcony.

Toward dawn, I woke to find that she was no longer beside me. She was always getting up to smoke. I thought I heard music from a transistor down the beach. There were fires set by surfers on the shoreline.

I sat up in the heat beneath the sheets and saw Jo leaning, nude and smoking, against the balcony of reddish wood.

"You okay?" I asked. She didn't hear. "Jo?"

She dropped the cigarette to the sand and climbed into bed, turning her back to me so that all I saw in the moonlight was the curve of her thighs.

I told her about Colony Records. I told her about *Amahl and the Night Visitors*. I told her about the tape.

"You think it got switched?" she asked.

"I guess we'll find out in the morning."

But in the morning, she was gone.

FRIDAY, AUGUST 24

61.

It was hot. Thick green flies hummed among torn cocktail napkins and the bottles strewn about the balcony. The screen door was open. The radio was on. It was Sunday. I rubbed whatever was left of sleep from my eyes, sat up, and looked for Jo.

The bed was empty.

I ran out to the balcony and watched waves crashing on the beach I hadn't seen the night before and looked down the cliff through the mist to the sand that ran unbroken, except for the rocks and the man with a stick and a dog, all the way to the shore.

Gulls screamed and picked at strands of seaweed and burned driftwood. There was nothing on the horizon, no line but just those black waves disappearing into mist.

She wasn't there.

The diary and tape were gone.

So was the Greyhound key.

A note on the bedside table read: "Let's break this thing wide open! Love, Jo."

At eight-thirty, I turned the bedside Wilco to *Annie Laurie Presents*. I heard cheerful chatter about James Mason, Laurence Olivier, and Wally Cox. "Seems Wally Cox is not only a great comedian but also a magician, if you've seen his latest soap commercial, dear ones," she said. "Well, Wally throws a cup of detergent and dirty clothes into a top-loading washer, then presto pulls the clothes out nicely clean. Some trick, dear ones! Oh, but I kid you, Wally. See you Friday! Kisses."

At first I thought that Jo had developed a cold or was upset or something. She had the Annie Laurie voice but it was different. I couldn't place it. When the time came for the call-in questions, I called the number that she'd given and got a busy signal. They called this segment the "Round Robin," and it was preceded by the sound effect of a bird chirping. Yeah, I know: stupid, but that's show business.

I was getting the busy signal, but I kept calling until her producer answered: *"Annie Laurie Presents."*

"This is Ben Fitzgerald. I'm a friend of Jo's."

"Who?"

"Jo Carnahan."

"So?"

"I need to talk to her. It's important that you put me through."

"I don't think you know what's going on, mister. . . ."

"Put me through."

"What's your question?"

"I need to talk to Jo."

"And I need to know your question."

So I told him.

Six minutes later, he flipped a switch and I was on:

"—morning, and welcome to *Annie Laurie Presents.* What's your name?"

"Ben Fitzgerald."

"Good morning, dear one. State your question."

"What do you get," I said, "when you cross an elephant with a rhinoceros?"

"I beg your pardon?" Annie Laurie said. "Sir, please turn your radio off."

I flipped the switch.

"I said, what do you get when you cross an elephant with a rhinoceros?"

"What does that have to do with—"

"You're not Jo."

"I'm Annie Laurie. And I'm not sure what this has to do with—"

"Marilyn Monroe was murdered," I said. "The Kennedys were involved. So was Captain James Hamilton of the LAPD, and no one wants to know the truth. There was no water glass. She didn't take the pills."

I went on for a while. I went on for a *long* while—until I realized I was talking into a void. They had cut me off. "Hello?"

I hung up and turned the radio back on, Annie Laurie saying: "—on good authority that Humphrey Bogart and Lauren Bacall will be at the gala premiere, to be held next Friday at Grauman's. A fine time will be had by all. And while we're discussing—"

I called the Ambassador Hotel and asked to be connected to Jo's room. The phone kept ringing, until—

Someone picked up.

I heard breathing, something rattling.

"Jo?"

Someone hung up.

"Jo."

62.

This is Sheila Dent from Panorama City," a woman said on WOLA as the cab drove me down Wilshire. "As a loyal listener, Miss Laurie, I'd like to thank you for the two times you mentioned Soupy Sales on your show recently. I am an avid Soupy fan and just love to hear about him."

"We *all* love Soupy, dear one," Annie said.

"I've heard that he will be starring in a new TV series called something O'Toole. Can you tell me if—"

I lit a cigarette.

Tomorrow would be—

You know.

The man at the front desk said that Ms. Carnahan was at WOLA in Burbank. She had been at the show all morning, he said. I told him it wasn't possible, that the woman who was now Annie Laurie was not Jo Carnahan. Annie Laurie had changed yet again. The man at the front desk said that he was happy to take a message, if I *cared* to leave a message. I said I did not: "I think she's here. *Someone's* here.

I need to see her. Call and tell her that it's Ben Fitzgerald and I need to see her."

"But, Mr. Fitzgerald," he said. "With all due respect, you're already here."

"What?"

"Look." He picked up the heavy reception book that sat on the desk and turned to the morning's entries. At 7:15 A.M., a Mr. Ben Fitzgerald had signed in. "He hasn't left," he said. "*You* haven't left."

I ran through the lobby to the elevator.

"Sir!" he shouted. He dropped the phone and stepped out from behind the desk.

Elevator: fifth floor. Fourth.

The stairs were to my left. I took them all the way to [redacted].

She was on the bed, her head turned toward the *puce* curtains that blew in over the window and the fire escape overlooking the pool and the beach. Her back was propped against the headboard, eyes staring unblinking at the mirror above the dresser, her usually coiffed black hair mussed like a wig that had shifted. Her makeup was smeared, a lipstick stain on her cheek. She wore those dark false eyelashes.

The Wilco on the bedside table was tuned to *Annie Laurie Presents.* Annie Laurie hadn't died. Annie Laurie was forever, the woman who was not Jo talking about Peter O'Toole, Maureen O'Hara, and Theodore Curphey. She quoted Curphey's findings:

"Miss Monroe had often expressed the wish to give up, withdraw, and even to die."

Beside the Wilco: a water glass stained with lipstick; two vials of Nembutal; a half-empty bottle of Canadian Club sitting next to the

Monroe diary, the bus locker key, the Sony reel-to-reel, flight records from Conners on Clover Field, and a handwritten note.

WOLA: "On more than one occasion in the past, when disappointed and depressed, Marilyn had made suicide attempts using sedative drugs. On these occasions, she had called for help and been rescued."

I read what Jo had written on the note:

"[redacted] and life. I don't know how I can face it anymore."

But what really got me, Doctor, was the postscript. Who writes a postscript to a suicide note? Jo did, apparently:

"P.S.," she wrote: "Hell-if-I-know."

She inhaled—a sharp rattling sound: the sound of Nembutal.

"Jo." I stepped forward. "Jesus," I said—and that was when he shot her.

Her head jerked violently to one side, blood shooting like water from a hose and covering the bedding. It spattered up at me, as if someone had thrown a bucket of paint.

The gamy smell of iron filled the room.

I looked up.

Captain James Hamilton raised his Smith & Wesson as he walked from the hall all the way to where I stood—tongue lolling in his mouth, hip cocked—and put the gun between my eyes. The chamber was so close that it separated into two chambers, his face looming behind, as if in extreme close-up, seen through a fish-eye lens. "Here," he said, taking the vial of pills from the table and holding it before my eyes. It blurred. "Have some."

"No."

He pointed the gun at my left foot and blew the tip off my big toe.

"God. Damn!" I shouted, hopping on my right foot, falling to the floor, staring up at the ceiling. "Damn."

"I know how to take away the hurt." He handed me that vial of pills, which was now (along with his hand) so much bigger than his body. His face seemed far away. The ceiling fan whirred like a halo behind it. "Here."

I didn't take the vial.

He hit my face with the gun and held it to my other foot.

"Okay." The vial trembled in my hands. I popped a yellow jacket.

"Another."

I did: the bitter taste in my mouth.

"And another."

After a while, everything started to blur.

"And this is where we started," I say. "I mean I've told you this already, Doc."

"Tell me again."

I felt that I'd spent hours, days, lying on the floor of this hotel with my head on the wood and my eyes open wide as the air came through the vent near my head. The whoosh was all I heard—until I heard the closing of the door, the keys in the lock, the footsteps on the floor stopping only when I turned to see the patent leather shoes beside my eyes, the stub of a cigarette dropped between them, burning.

And then there was the gun.

"Captain Hamilton put the gun to my neck," I say. "He forced me to write a suicide note. I grabbed the gun."

"You grabbed—?"

"—his arm was in a sling," I say. "And then I shot him."

My eardrums were blown out, the world underwater, but even so I could hear the pounding on the door, the LAPD, hotel security, and bellmen spilling in.

"Memo to newsmen everywhere," Annie Laurie's voice: "Reporters who want to interview Tony Randall and ask personal queries had better be in good shape. Randall conducts most of his New York interviews at the Gotham Health Club while exercising. And in the Long, Deep Sigh Department—"

The window over the fire escape was just above the radiator. I climbed through it and down the metal stairs, on my way out to the reservoir.

63.

Now, these are the truly damning pictures—the ones that show me stumbling along Wilshire, my right hand covering one eye to stop the street from doubling as the bellmen and cops follow, dark blotches on the sidewalks.

And everything in slow motion.

I tried to hail a cab.

The light was blue and yellow and the sun was high, and everyone was gone. I could hardly raise my head. Everything was too heavy. Including my fingers. The world was too much. Everything—

There were two cabs. And two drivers.

"The reservoir," I said, climbing into the back.

"Jesus, mister," the drivers said. "What the hell happened to you?"

"I stubbed my toe."

"On an industrial blender?"

"Just go!"

I needed to stay awake.

I couldn't stay awake.

Now you lean back in your chair and light another cigarette. "Hang on a second," you say. "What did you do with the tape?"

"Left it at Jo's."

"You're lying."

"No."

"Oh?" You press STOP and change the tape. You take the roll from the reel-to-reel and rummage through the pile of boxes until you find Spool #13, marked "CAB DRIVER 9/19/62."

You thread the tape through the machine and press PLAY:

"Guy was knocked out of his brain," the driver said. "Bleeding like a stuck pig and couldn't stand. He told me to shut up and 'take me to Lake Hollywood Reservoir,' he said. He could hardly stay awake, and I thought I saw a gun coming out of his pants. And he was carrying a tape."

"A tape?"

"Some kind of reel-to-reel. Hell, I don't know *why*. I just know that he was carrying it like God's own—"

You press STOP. "You took it from Jo's room."

"I didn't."

"Tell the truth."

"The truth is the pain is bad, Doc: Give me a Novril."

"Tell me what happened first. Then you can have whatever you want."

"The truth is—"

"Hang on," you say. "Let me change the reel."

64.

The truth is that, yes, I took the tape. I took the diary, too, and carried them both to the street and hailed a cab. But halfway to the reservoir, the drivers got mouthy. I saw it coming. They were smoking and kept glancing up at me in the rearview mirror. The mirror was going double but I could see them giving what I've come to call "The Look."

"You're not one of those film stars, now, are you?" they asked.

"No one."

"You look familiar."

"I get that a lot."

"I think I know who you are. It's coming to me, yeah—"

"You going to drive?"

"Just making conversation."

"Sure, well, here's some conversation: You know how people ask, 'Is there a gun in your pocket, or are you just happy to see me?' " I asked.

"Sure."

I took Captain Hamilton's gun from my pocket. "I'm not happy to see you."

Lake Hollywood Reservoir is just below the Hollywood sign up in the Hills. We took the freeway to the Barham exit and then Cahuenga to Lake Hollywood Drive.

I told the drivers to park near the gate.

We got out of the car. I walked them up the service road through the vegetation to the base of the dam. In the woods that surrounded it I held the drivers at gunpoint and told them to take off their clothes. They kicked off shoes, then socks. They unbuttoned their shirts.

I did, too.

I put their clothes on and left them naked, taking my clothes and the wallet and the keys back to the cab. I drove in the hat and the clothes that I had stolen and stopped at a Rexall. I bought ten Benzedrine inhalers and cracked two open and balled the paper up and swallowed. Well, the uppers didn't mix with what I'd taken, but what choice did I have? I needed to stay awake. I could hear my heart beat on the radio. I tasted metal in my throat.

The sun burned past the buildings. The buildings burned, too, though maybe this was only the reflection. I kept hearing sirens. Were they police or fire? Things were creeping from behind the street signs, even as the signs themselves were changing. I couldn't see the word STOP. I must have run through red lights. People on the streets kept waving at me, which I thought meant something terrible. Did they see that I was burning? Did they know that I had killed a man?

It was only later that I realized I was driving a cab.

65.

I parked outside Verona Gardens and went straight through the lobby up the stairs. I was looking for Max. I was going to take Max. It wasn't far to the border, and if I hurried I could make it. Then I could disappear. The door to 203 was ajar.

The place had been ransacked. The TV was on. Steam came from the bathroom past the closet filled with hangers. The bathroom door was open, neon strips bracketing a fogged mirror. Water shrieked through the hooked sink faucet and hissed from the shower. The toilet was open and running. The rug on the floor was spattered with blood.

A porkpie hat sat on the nap.

I pulled the curtain back.

My wife lay in the bathtub, naked and hogtied with hose. A sock had been stuffed in her mouth. Her skin was stained with broad burns from the water, which I turned off.

I pulled the sock from her mouth.

"Jesus—"

"They broke down the door."

"Who's *they*?"

"People. Looking for Max."

"Where's Max?"

"With Johnny."

"*Where?*"

"Santa Anita."

"Did you tell them that?"

"They hurt me."

"Rose. Did you tell them?"

I ran to her phone and called: "Operator," I said, "we need help. In Verona on the Boulevard. She's . . . Man, she's really . . . Jesus. Burned—"

She wanted me to leave her.

She told me to find Max.

I picked up the hat.

That's how you found the fingerprints.

66.

I took two more tubes from the glove compartment and broke them and swallowed the strips. The metal spread through my blood again, coating the back of my throat. I kept swallowing. I wanted to wash it out, but I didn't have a water glass.

The fire started up inside, but outside it was gone, replaced by sudden storms. Lightning danced as I drove to Santa Anita. I never saw it cut the sky, just the black clouds booming behind the Santa Monicas. It was secondhand evidence, like a shadow on a wall instead of a person walking.

But people were walking everywhere. They were waving, too.

I parked and, well, didn't have an umbrella—or a hat, thanks to the pie—and by the time I made it through the gate and bought a racing form, my suit was soaked. I figured I needed it. It cut the metal out.

I went up to the main line, diary and tape in hand, the beer stands and the monitors, the haze of smoke, men in straw hats and bad shorts, losing tickets on the floor, tellers behind the windows.

I found Johnny and Max in the ticket line and pretended to read the racing form as I watched the gangster spread a sheaf of Hamiltons at the window: "Five dimes on six to show in the second."

Johnny opened his black umbrella and walked with Max into the grandstand apron, toward the stretch, and sat on one of the benches. I lit a Kent and walked into the sea of bobbing umbrellas as the horses filed out to the gate.

"Johnny," I said.

He flicked his cigarette, still burning, to the ground, and looked up, giving me that Mafia stare.

"Dad!" Max shouted.

Johnny smiled. "You don't give up, do you?"

"It's like Davy Crockett said: Be sure you're right, then go ahead."

"You're not Davy Crockett," he said. "What are you doing here?"

My hand was in my pocket. "Your girlfriend is burned in the bathtub. She said you were here. They were looking for Max."

"Who?"

"The people who hurt her."

"LAPD," he said.

"How do you—?"

"On the one hand you have the Chicago outfit, Ben. On the other hand you have the LAPD. One is trying to protect the Kennedys. The other is trying to fuck them. Guess which one is on your side?"

"He isn't wearing a hat," I said.

"What?"

"The man who hurt my wife isn't wearing a hat. And he's here. He must be. She said—"

He looked around. "All these umbrellas—"

The nasal track announcer's voice came over tinny speakers: "Dagger's Point still in front, Dagger's Point by a length and a half, here comes Bullet Proof on the outside, Dagger's Point coming after him—"

People were standing. They were shouting. You could shoot someone in that noise and no one would hear.

"Wait a second!" Johnny stood. He shouted, too. He had won on Dagger's Point. Max sat quietly staring into his lap. The crowd pressed in as I stood on the bench and looked over the umbrellas and saw nothing except Johnny leading Max back to the ticket window.

I ran after them, tripping on a stair, and when I stood I saw the man.

Cagney sat under a black umbrella at the edge of the stairs to the right.

He didn't have his porkpie hat, but his umbrella followed me as I walked to the window—and put the gun to my son's head.

You need to change the tape again.

"Are we almost done?"

"You tell me. *You're* the one who kidnapped your son."

"I didn't."

"That's not what the *Mirror* said."

"The *Mirror* lies."

"Oh? They said—do I need to quote?—'a deranged drugged man put a gun to his son's head at Santa Anita—' "

"To stop them from hurting him the way they hurt my wife."

"*You* hurt your wife. You were stoned."

"—trying to stay awake."

"You hurt Max, too."

"No."

"You *threatened* to."

"To get him out of there."

"—gun pointing to his temple, left hand hooked under his neck. You *punched*—"

"He fell."

"—was *bleeding*."

"Look," I said. "I tried to stop it."

67.

Umbrellas rippled in the stands and men ducked and fell in the lines that snaked from the ticket windows. They were screaming. Well, that was my impression. It's hard for me to piece it all together, since time changed in those few moments. The drug wasn't helping. Everything happened in seconds but the seconds kept stretching. A hundred different things unspooled at once, like drama dioramas playing out across the track; you could rewind the film, and each time you would see something new:

STOP, REWIND, PLAY.

Yes, I grabbed my son and held him. Yes, I put the gun to his temple, and yes, I had my hand around his neck and Johnny reached for his gun and Cagney reached for his, and I think I said one of those clichéd things like "Don't move or I'll shoot!" or "One false move and he's dead!"

I led Max to the parking lot as screams and cheering filled the track, and when I tripped he fell straight to the ground.

. . .

Calm down, calm down, I told myself as I parked the cab at a gas station near Evansville. There were oil stains like bats on the cement and a service island with pumps painted pastel green. I brought Max to the restroom. It smelled of urine and chlorine. The faucet shrieked as I washed his bloody face and took his shirt off and rinsed and wrung it in the sink. It was still wet, so I carried it as I led him shirtless back into the lot.

I swear I saw a flash come from an El Dorado parked at an angle along the belled fence facing the Tastee Freez. I turned and looked behind me as we passed the car and I swore I saw another flash come from the back.

But there was nothing.

It wasn't long before we were outside Mission Viejo, but the streets weren't clearly marked. I was on the back roads, passing hotels and the gas stations that had been abandoned when the highway was first built. The world is changing: You know that, Doc. Gray fluorescence bloomed in convenience stores and red neon reflected in electric waves on the streets that looked like oil.

I was falling asleep. I pulled out an inhaler and swallowed the strips, but this time the fire and the metal were gone. I nodded off, crossing the center divide near Encinitas when the semi blew its horn, and I looked up just in time to see the big rig looming, blades of rain like translucent grass in the lights—and it's true what they say: Everything slows. I even had time to say, aloud, "You're doing okay," which woke Max as I yanked the wheel to the right, so hard that I went into the ditch.

"Shit," I said, climbing from the car. The cars hummed past.

I heard sirens.

"That's no good, Dad," Max said.

"I know: car's stuck."

"I mean your language," he said, stepping toward the road and raising his right hand, flagging down a car.

"Don't, Max."

"Why?"

"No one knows we're here."

68.

The hotel was one of those creaky Victorian structures they call California Gingerbread. There was a wooden porch with a swing that drifted in the wind. The steps that led to the WELCOME mat at the front door belled in the middle. Turns out it wasn't a hotel so much as a bed-and-breakfast in a part of Titusville now visited only by people who had gotten lost or, like us, had too few options.

I rang the bell.

The owner was one Carol McFadden, a plump widow in a nightgown and fringed cap that covered her curlers. Traces of cream slicked her skin and smelled of cough drops. She greeted us at the front door, yawning, having already been to bed. But she was "glad to see" us, she said. "It must be good to get out of the rain."

"Sure is," I said, shaking off in the front parlor. A front desk with a brass bell and a guest book fronted the side of a staircase that led up to the rooms.

"How did you find us?"

"The truth, ma'am," I said, "is we got lost."

"That seems to be the only way these days. Just the two of you?" she said brightly, stepping behind the desk.

"Sure enough."

She frowned at Max. "Your boy okay?"

"He fell off his bike."

"Sorry to hear it, son." She looked back up at me. "Deposit in cash?"

Shit, I had no money. Somehow I'd forgotten that.

"Sure," Max said, taking a wad of bills from his plastic cowboy wallet and handing it to the woman.

It was Monopoly money.

The woman looked at me. "Surely the boy is joking."

"Wait!" He dug into his wallet again. "Sorry."

He handed her a hundred-dollar bill.

"Well," she said. "I'll be!"

"Where did you get that?" I asked my son.

"Horse books," he said.

We signed in. I used the names "John and Al Rawlston."

"Is there any place to eat around here?" I asked.

"There's an all-night café about ten miles back, but you don't exactly look in the mood for another trip. Hmm, I didn't hear a car, either."

"We parked around the block."

"You could have used the lot."

"If it's all right with you, ma'am, we'll leave the car where it is. We really just need a shower and sleep."

She hesitated. "Tell you what," she said. "I'll cook you something up myself."

"You sure? It's late."

"Don't mind," she said. "I like the company."

We went up to dry off in the room. There were two single beds facing a Zenith, a double window looking out over a fire escape with a view of the parking lot below and, past it, the wharfs and the docks off the beach. The room was decorated like a dollhouse, with pointless small tables, lacy pillows, and pastels.

It was like being inside an Easter egg.

I put the tape and the diary on the bedside table. Max took a bath and I took a shower and we climbed into the bed, wet clothes over the shower rod, and watched the TV that hardly worked. Well, it was past sign-off anyway. They had already shown the American flag.

"So what did you do with the tape?" you say.

"You're like a broken record, Doc."

"Because you're not telling the truth."

"I don't know what you mean."

You stop the current tape, take one of the others from the unending pile, cue it up, and hit PLAY:

"—called the cops." It was Carol McFadden's voice. "Well, they were asking—"

STOP. REWIND. PLAY:

"It did strike me as strange," Carol says, "that this fellow with the son was so interested in listening to some silly tape, but what can I say? Maybe he was a music fan. I like 101 Strings myself. Do you?"

"Can't say that I know them. Please continue."

"Well, you should hear 'Gypsy Campfires.' You haven't heard a thing until you've heard 'Gypsy Campfires.' Well, I try to be helpful. It was my late husband's machine. I don't even know how to work it, and I wasn't sure it *did* work, but this gentleman just seemed so *keen* on it. That's all I can say. I've never felt that way about music, have you?"

"Now, please—"

"It wasn't music. That's the strange thing. At least if it *was*, it was like no music I've ever heard. Well, I heard him listening to this, and some of it—!"

"What?"

"Well, I can't be sure, but . . . sighs. And moans. Well, if the man hadn't had his young son with him, I could have sworn."

"What?"

"It was the sound of carnal love."

There are three distinct sections on the tape, Doctor. I am not sure why I think there are three sections, but they seem to reflect different times.

The first is just sex: loud and vocal. The less said about this the better, as I'm sure you can imagine it.

The rest of the tape lasts about sixty minutes and was recorded, I think, on the afternoon of August 4 and then again in the early morning hours of August 5. During the first twenty minutes, you can hear Marilyn and Eunice Murray talking.

"Marilyn?" the housekeeper says. "He won't go away. He's outside."

"Tell him I'm not here."

"He *knows* you're here."

"Tell him I'm sleeping."

Shouting.

"He won't believe you. He's upset. You never sleep. He needs to see you."

"Well, then, tell him to wait. Tell him—"

About five minutes later, you can hear Marilyn and Kennedy talking. It's not always clear. The sounds seem to come from a long way off, as if the interaction took place far from the transmitter in Monroe's closet. See, the quality is poor. Listen, however, to what happens when you reach 1406. At this precise spot, Marilyn says what is almost certainly "promised me." Rewind a few times, and you'll hear the "you":

"You promised me."

This is followed by Kennedy saying, "I promised you nothing."

"You [inaudible] me," she says.

I am sure the missing word here is "fucked." Though I do not expect the word that I have just written to survive. It will no doubt be crossed out, as it most likely is as you are reading [redacted]

"I feel passed around!" She sounds agitated, drugged, or drunk. "I feel used! I feel like a piece of meat!"

At 1506 (pay attention, now—there is a lot of static), you will hear Kennedy say, "Where is it?"

Marilyn screams something.

"It *has* to be here."

The sound quality is poor. As the people move about the bedroom, now near to and now far from the mics, the quality fluctuates. What is clear is the fact that the voices grow louder, angrier, until it's obvious that they are arguing. At, say, 1708, Kennedy sounds shrill, like a querulous old lady as he asks repeatedly, "Where is it? Where the fuck is it?"

You will notice that this portion of the tape ends with the sound of a slamming door.

From 1897 to 1945, the tape is silent. You will hear only white noise, a few clicking sounds, no clues, no evidence. Believe me. I have heard it. The silence is so long you may be tempted to turn the tape off, thinking it is over. Do not do this. Instead, fast-forward to the point at which the counter turns from 1430 to 1431. Here, you will hear feedback, an odd clicking sound, and voices.

I believe they are the voices of Robert Kennedy, Peter Lawford, and Marilyn Monroe.

Kennedy is angrier and louder now. Marilyn sounds drunk or stoned. She is probably both.

In the fifty-five minutes that follow, from 2123 to 3001, three things are clear. The first is that, right off the bat, Kennedy says, "We have to know. We can make any arrangements that you want, but we must find it. It's important to the family."

They must have gotten close to the rice-sized transmitter, because you hear a clacking on the tape, which I insist is the sound of hangers moving back on the rack in the closet, clothes being shuffled around as Kennedy and Lawford search for the bug that, they believe, was installed at Marilyn's request. They had their own bug; they had their own tape. But Marilyn's?

They are still searching.

Next through the static is what I can only call a flopping sound, followed again by that Kennedy old-lady voice and Lawford saying, "Calm down. Calm—"

"Get out!" Marilyn shouts. "Get the fuck out of the—"

"Calm down!"

Here, from 2104 to 2540, you'll hear crashing, then whispered comforting sounds, as if someone is putting a child to bed.

Then there is a long silence.

The last part of this tape is a conversation, clearly heard, between Lawford and Kennedy.

"I'm going back to San Francisco," Kennedy says.

"San Francisco," says Lawford. "What about—"

"Call once I'm out of the area."

"You can't just."

"I will. I can. You'll call."

There are elisions after this, as there are elisions everywhere, missing pieces of the tape, missing pieces of the puzzle and the diary and the story. Missing lives. For the next thirty minutes, it sounds as if the tape is being turned on and then off. At 4106 you will hear a steady clicking sound, followed by a sort of hollow whoosh. Other than that, and the sound of the door slamming finally shut, there is nothing.

Nothing, that is, until the phone rings at 5401. The sound is abrupt. The phone rings five times, and someone picks it up. You can hear the vague clatter of plastic against plastic. No one speaks. Someone gently puts the phone in its receiver.

Someone has finally hung up.

69.

Now your own tape runs. The smoke from your cigarette rises to the ceiling, where it hangs around the bulb; the fan has stopped. You blink, then crush the cigarette into the ashtray.

"Where is the tape?" you ask.

"I burned it."

"Then why did you give me instructions?"

"I don't know what you mean."

"You kept saying, 'You will find, you will hear.' You're giving me *instructions*."

"It's a form of speech."

"It's not a form you use about something that no longer exists."

"I had to get rid of it. Well, now I knew the ending. Why keep it in the world, you know? And, anyway, they came for us. I knew they would."

There was a knock at our door, so I wrapped a towel around my waist, turned off the tape, and answered it. Carol McFadden stood in the hall carrying a silver tray covered with a series of white napkins. "I hope," she said, "I'm not interrupting anything."

"No." I held the door shut.

"Well, may I come in?"

I turned to Max. He was under the covers, smiling.

I opened the door, and the woman saw my towel and jumped as if I had given her a shock, but professionally proceeded to place the tray on the table near the bed anyway.

"Turkey sandwich on rye with cheese, potato salad, to-maytas from my garden," she said, unveiling her concoctions. "Snack Packs for dessert: sorry, no homemade." She smiled. "I did what I could."

"We really appreciate it," I said.

"Don't mention it. So nice to see a father and son spending some time together. All too often that sort of connection is lost in this day and age."

"I agree."

"Too bad about the young feller's nose."

"Thanks. He'll be okay."

She was halfway out the door when she stopped, turned, and looked back. "Good night, Mr. Fitzgerald."

The door shut quietly behind her.

"How did she know my name?" I asked.

"What, Dad?"

I ran to the window and looked over the fire escape.

The B. F. Fox van idled under a faint pool of streetlight.

So that was when we left: We ran in the dark down the street that ended in the beach, a boardwalk and a pier leading out to the ocean. You couldn't see the sea, but the waves were loud at the edge where a paved road led past trash cans and signs saying NO DUMPING. The smell of rank fish and salt and seaweed was strong. Along the shoreline I saw fires and, ten yards out, surfers and the lights of fishing boats on the surface.

Sirens sounded in the distance.

I turned, still holding Max's hand, and saw a train of red and blue lights streaming down the main street.

"Come on." I pulled Max into the sand that made it hard to run. We stumbled together as the cruisers pulled up to the shore road and parked, lights rolling. The bobbing bluish flashlights were all I saw as the cops headed down to the beach.

I slipped into the sloped sand under the pier, the pilings slick with algae and seaweed, darkened in rings where the surf rose and fell.

"What are we doing?"

"We have to be quiet."

"Okay." Max reached for my hand. He gave me his thimble.

The flashlight beams bobbed, revealing tufts of sand grass, dead crabs, and cracked gray clamshells.

Cheering came from one of the fires along the shore.

The beams all turned toward the sound, then went back to crawling raggedly along the sand.

One of them darted to us.

I clutched Max's hand.

I don't remember how long we waited, Doc, but after the flashlights disappeared, cars pulling away, we walked to the fires where the surfers sat on boards and driftwood shirtless and smoking or playing guitars and drinking from a shared bottle of Scotch. Empties littered the sand.

"I use your fire?" I asked them.

"Sure. What for?"

I held the Monroe diary up. "*Ulysses*," I said, and tossed it in.

The pages of that sad book curled in the flames, ignited, then blackened and drifted up into the night air like bats. I watched them float in the smoke and the sparks. Then I tossed in the tape, which curled and melted, until—

"Dad," Max said.

"What, sport?"

He didn't answer.

"Sport?" I turned toward him. "Oh my God."

SATURDAY, AUGUST 25

70.

I know that I am slurring now. I might have had too many. You ask me the same questions. You ask me to repeat myself, but I am trying to stop the spinning. I shouldn't have swallowed them all, but I did. The point is they will tell you I am crazy. They will tell you I'm an addict and can't be trusted. They held back my arms on both sides; I couldn't struggle. I kicked. My legs were the only things that I could move, until the floor was upended and the lightbulb on the ceiling passed over my eyes like a star, and my head hit the floor with a crack.

All I could see was the fan spinning slowly on the ceiling as they rolled my right sleeve up and took the tourniquet from the table and tied it on my arm and pulled it tight and the next thing I knew my eyes were bright and blinking against the light shining down, blood surging as a wave spread like darkness over the sun, an eclipse in my blood slowly blanketing my body with warmth and a peace that I had never known.

And everything in slow motion.

"Wait a second," you say. "Where were you?"

"The hospital."

"What happened to Max?"

"I brought him there. Well, he had all the symptoms. The itchy chin. The sound in his chest. The coughing and the sweat. It was an asthma attack, Doc. So what was I gonna do? They arrested me when I arrived—for assault and kidnapping. They wouldn't let me see him. They called my wife."

"Your wife."

"They found her in the tub."

Was I in that room for a month? I don't know. The days telescoped and expanded, like an accordion. Einstein was wrong: Time isn't relative. It's a box-shaped musical instrument of the bellows-driven free-reed aerophone family. Someone told me that I had checked myself in for the same sort of pill addiction that Marilyn had had. Like her, I had a taste for yellow jackets and, later, the black Novril.

They injected me. They fed me Novril, and kept feeding me the Novril, until they brought me here—wherever "here" is, Doc: the gray-green room with no windows and a metal door. A bare bulb on a ceiling fan over the long table. The reel-to-reel, a stack of tapes, an ashtray, and your pack of cigarettes. That and, of course, the box with the large label reading "Fitzgerald, Ben, Psych Eval" containing what you call "the evidence":

1. The Smith & Wesson
2. A vial of Nembutal
3. A piece of notebook paper reading "Chalet 52" and "July 28"
4. A stained manila folder containing a number of 8 × 10 photographs
5. *Amahl and the Night Visitors*
6. A bag of ashes
7. A new red MEMORIES diary

You pick up No. 6 and dump it on the table. Gray puffs rise. You stir through the ashes recovered from the fire, removing the last remaining page. You hold it up and read the words out loud:

The doorbell rang then. Pat was out by the pool she was still mad. "You can't hold a press conference," she said.

"But sure I can. I'm going to blow this whole thing wide open."

"Marilyn, it's the craziest thing," she said. "You can't keep the baby."

You put the pages down. "Well?"

"What?"

"You didn't tell the whole story. You left the main thing out."

"I don't know what you mean."

"Finish the diary, Ben," you say. "Tell me what else you think happened."

THE BOOK OF SECRETS
by Ben Fitzgerald

71.

Forgive me but it was all I ever wanted," Marilyn had written. "I tried so many times but never with results and always with pain, well once I almost died but this will be different and will change everything, the one who will have the things I never had and see the things I never saw and be loved and safe and sane and mine.

"[redacted], forgive me: [redacted]."

The lacunae here are "Bobby" and "you're a daddy again."

Arthur Miller once said that a baby would have been, for Marilyn, "a crown with a thousand diamonds." But when she found herself pregnant by the attorney general, it wasn't a crown. It was why she died. It was why Sinatra had taken Monroe to the Cal-Neva Lodge, why she had been drugged and, worse, why the photos were taken. If she refused to do what they were asking her, the photos were evidence they could use against her: She was nothing but a whore, like the word that she'd read on the window.

She had threatened to take all her secrets to the media. She had threatened more than once to call a press conference. And now she was going to have a baby. Which might have been the reason behind the series of phone calls from the unidentified woman (Ethel Kennedy?) the night before Monroe died:

"You stay away from Bobby," she had said, knowing even then that the General's eighth child was growing in the body of the film star.

All she'd ever wanted was that crown of diamonds, but why torture yourself with hellos?

Now you keep saying, "Finish the story. Write what you know." But are you CIA or LAPD? Do you want evidence against the Kennedys or a reason to kill me?

Whatever: The pages from the logs at Conners helicopter at Clover Field in Santa Monica—the ones I'd found on Jo's table—clearly showed the record of two helicopter flights. The first, from San Francisco, had landed at 1:16 P.M. on August 4 at Stage 18 of the 20th Century-Fox lot near the Beverly Hilton. The second had flown out of Santa Monica just after midnight on August 5, heading to (where else?) San Francisco.

So what does this mean?

It means that Bobby *could* have left Gilroy on Saturday, flying from San Francisco to the Fox lot after lunch and then heading to see Marilyn. It meant he could have returned to Gilroy in time for prayers on Sunday. But Marilyn was found dead after midnight. Why did the second flight leave L.A. for San Francisco almost twelve hours after the first flight arrived? Maybe Bobby didn't get what he wanted from Marilyn in the afternoon. So maybe he *returned* to her house that night—perhaps with Dr. Greenson, perhaps with Peter Lawford. And what happened then?

Maybe they administered either an enema (which would have explained the purplish congestion in the colon) or a hot shot, which might have explained the bruise.

We had, after all, found a large bruise on her left hip, a bruise that must have resulted from something that had happened on the night that she died. Maybe, drunk and high on pills, she was stumbling about the scattered scripts of that small bedroom, telephone in hand, bumping up against one or another of the pieces of furniture, or falling and hitting her hip against—what?—the bed? But I think it's far more likely that someone *inflicted* that bruise.

Noguchi thought so, too, for the record.

And now it is—

Well, I'm not sure. There are no windows, and the lights are off, but from the paper that you left behind, I can see that things are calming down. It was Black Saturday. Now it's only Lonely Monday: "the dismantling of offensive weapons is an important contribution to peace and . . . the governments of the world can turn their attention to the need to end the arms race," the president said.

And all that.

I can't read the rest.

I don't expect this to survive, but listen: My name won't show up in the obituaries. My life will be erased, the photos of my death ending up among the suicides and homicides and accidental overdoses in *The Book of the Unknown Dead.*

And now I'm wondering if the moment is coming when I will close my eyes and the things that seem real bleed into what can't be. That's the second you know you are slipping which is what I feel now a slow slipping. I want to write it out, what I remember, but am falling asleep leap a leap and so I won't forget:

72.

CASE NO.: 81136

DECEDENT NAME: UNKNOWN

CONTENTS:

1. A MONOGRAMMED SHIRT
2. A MONOPOLY THIMBLE
3. A SUICIDE NOTE: "*Take care of Max for me. Tell him that I loved him. Tell him that whatever else his father did, he loved his son.*"

LOCATION: BOX 35, ROW 33-D

ACKNOWLEDGMENTS

For support before, during, and after: Lani Adler, Josh Baker, Julie Baker, Thomas H. Cook, NYPD Detective Glenn Cunningham (retired), Ellen Datlow, Dennis Dermody, Klara Glowczewska, Scott Heim, Gail Horwood, John Huey, Clive Irving, Sue James, Bucky Keady, Dave C. Keady, Jim Kelly, Cindi Leive, Michael Lowenthal, Rob Minkoff, Scott Mowbray, Brothers Mueller, Martha Nelson, Sara Nelson, Winifred Ormond, Melissa Parrish, Otto Penzler, Daniel Silk, Geraldine Somers, Byron Stinson, Cyndi Stivers, Susan Terner, Kristin van Ogtrop, Craig Wright, Hanya Yanagihara, and Token Yee.

Special thanks and an enormous debt of gratitude to Richard Pine, who saw something in many early efforts and never stopped believing; Sarah Hochman, whose inspired edits and steady course saved me from myself in this; David Rosenthal, Aileen Boyle, Brian Ulicky, and their colleagues at Blue Rider Press and Penguin USA; and Philip Friedman, for absolutely everything.

SPILT GRAPE JUICE